Sorry,
You're Not
my Type

Sorry, You're my Not Type

Sudeep nagarkar

RANDOM HOUSE INDIA

Published by Random House India in 2014
Fourteenth impression in 2015

Random House Publishers India Private Limited
7th Floor, Infinity Tower C, DLF Cyber City
Gurgaon–122 002
Haryana, India

Random House Group Limited
20 Vauxhall Bridge Road
London SW1V 2SA
United Kingdom

978 81 8400 490 8

Typeset in Adobe Garamond Pro by SwaRadha Typesetting, New Delhi

Printed and bound in India by Replika Press Private Limited

A PENGUIN RANDOM HOUSE COMPANY

To VAYU

Jo tumhari neende udaaye,
Khwaab hai sacha wahi!
Jo tumhari neendo me aaye,
Khwaab woh sacha nahi!

Contents

Prologue

We all have dreams. But if we want those dreams to come true, we have to strive really hard. They too had a dream. They too had strived hard to achieve their dream. But would they see the dream turn into reality? Only time would tell.

It was the evening of the grand finale. The atmosphere was abuzz with activity and the excitement was palpable. Students from Delhi University had gathered in the campus lawns to watch the various bands perform.

This year the event looked bigger, better, and even more promising than the one held the previous year. There was an air of nervous anticipation. As the emcee called the band from Rajhans College on stage, everyone cheered loudly. By then a huge crowd had gathered in the lawns. All of a sudden, the lights went off and silence filled the air.

We have waited for this moment for long. Finally our time has arrived! We need to give our best if we want a shot at winning. I just hope Yuvi hasn't taken drugs. We can't afford to take chances today, Vikrant thought to himself and turned to face Yuvi.

Yuvi stood there confidently. He had dreamt of this day since childhood. He planted a kiss on his girlfriend Kashish's mouth. He considered it a sign of good luck.

As their lips parted, she said, 'I am sure you will steal everyone's hearts tonight. I feel so jealous.'

Yuvi gave her a smile, which, like always, sent shivers down her spine. She was his moral support and he always wanted her beside him, cheering on the band. Though she was not involved with the band physically, her mental support always boosted their confidence.

The stage was set. All three of them were ready to take the spotlight. They knew how important this was to kick-start their career. It was more important for them to secure a win for their college's reputation since the cup had eluded them for the past few years. The competition was stiff but the cultural team of Rajhans had full faith in their band.

'I am ready guys. I know we can do it. Let's make the most of it,' Anamika muttered in her sexy voice while walking towards the stage.

They looked at each other and exchanged nervous smiles. As they took their positions and stood facing the crowd, the spotlights fell on them. The crowd erupted in cheer and applause.

Anamika, the dancer of the band, looked gorgeous in a little black dress. There was not a single guy in the crowd who was not fantasizing about her. Vikrant, the drummer, was a perfectionist. Yuvi was probably the best guitarist and vocalist any college could have. The trio was the perfect combination of looks and talent.

Strumming the guitar, Yuvi started singing the most popular song of the band. Slowly, all the students in the playground swirled to the beats of the music. Yuvi had the potential to mesmerize everyone and he poured his heart out in the performance. Anamika and Vikrant encouraged the crowd to sway their hands in the air. Everything seemed picture perfect and the confidence with which the band was performing, it seemed like Rajhans had almost won the trophy.

But none had anticipated the disaster that was awaiting them. Just when everything seemed perfect, the mic stopped working and a cord of the electric guitar came apart! Yuvi kept blaming the sound technician for the bizarre set up. No matter how hard the trio tried, things never came back on track. The performance was called off by the judges and the crowd started booing them off. All their hopes were shattered as Yuvi and the other group members walked off the stage with their heads hung in shame.

A feeling of hopelessness engulfed them. They had waited for this day for so long and had practiced for hours after college. Neither of them had imagined this to be the end result. They couldn't believe what was happening to them.

'How could they do this? This is not fair. We should be given another chance. It was the grand finale and the judges can't be so biased. What's our bloody fault?' Anamika shouted in frustration.

'The technician was an asshole! How the fuck did he not check our equipment before the performance? I sense something fishy,' said Vikrant.

And the blame game continued. Yuvi hadn't said a word till then. He still couldn't believe what had happened a few minutes back. A tear came rolling down his cheek. Though he had taken drugs that evening, he was well in control of the situation and had given one of the finest performances of his life before everything went haywire. Both Anamika and Vikrant were voicing their frustration loudly and Yuvi's silence was killing them.

'Will you speak up, for God's sake?' Anamika screamed.

Yuvi was still quiet and didn't look up until Anamika shook him by his shoulders.

'Can you just leave me alone, you bitch? It's all because of you. Who told you to fuck it up? You and your boyfriend messed everything up. It's all because of him. Oops sorry, it's all because of you. Just get lost.'

Yuvi walked off in anger. Vikrant ran after him and tried to stop him from leaving. Vikrant was confused and upset with what was happening around him. He wanted to calm down the two and resolve the issue.

'Yuvi, at least listen to me. How are you so sure it was because of him?' Vikrant screamed.

Yuvi stopped and looked back in anger. 'Do you think I am a fucking fool? I saw him talking with the technicians a few seconds before our show. He obviously messed everything up. He had told her he will screw it all up and he did.' Saying this he walked away. Vikrant gave up. He realized the situation was out of his hand and there was nothing he could do to pacify Yuvi.

Anamika's sour relationship with her boyfriend had cost them big time! It was probably going to be the last performance of their lives.

The hopes that they had shared, the dreams that they had seen—all of it was suddenly swept out of their lives like dust on the floor. Anamika was heartbroken by Yuvi's words. She tried to regain composure and, collecting her thoughts, messaged her ex-boyfriend.

I have given up on my dream because I don't want my group to suffer. You envied me, but why my group? Why my band? You think you have achieved all that you wanted and can now stop me from achieving mine? I am not a girl who will sit back and cry. Do whatever you want. I give a damn. You have no balls. Fuck you bastard.

Rajhans College had lost the competition and the trophy too. Yuvi didn't bother to wait for the results and left with his girlfriend. Vikrant was speechless and didn't know how to react while Anamika sat alone trying to understand what had just happened. She felt like she was trapped in a cage. She sensed the end was near—the end of their band VAYU!

That Seductive Night

Mia Bella, Hauz Khaz Village, Delhi
14th September 2013, 10 pm

'No amount of coffee, no amount of crying, no amount of whiskey, no amount of wine… I gotta have you,' sang the mesmerzing voice while I chilled with my friend Sakshi at the Mia Bella pub.

Sakshi, one of my best friends, was effortlessly beautiful. She was of medium height, with narrow shoulders, slender legs, and a tiny waist. She had an air of confidence about her. Her jet-black curls blew in the evening breeze like the black waves that blow over the ocean on stormy nights. Her fair skin glowed and her eyes had the spark that could set forests ablaze. But her best feature was her smile. She could light up any party with just her smile. I admired her as a friend since she had always stood by me whenever I needed someone. Our friendship was over a decade old but we couldn't meet very often due to the long distance between us. I had little clue about good places to eat in Delhi, so I had asked Sakshi to decide where to go.

When we reached Mia Bella around 10 pm, Sakshi told me that we needed to climb three floors. I pleaded with Sakshi that I was tired, but she remained stubborn and took me upstairs. By the time we reached the rooftop, I had a big smile on my face. All my tiredness evaporated into thin air. It had a terrific view of the lake and the cold breeze made it feel even more amazing. I hugged Sakshi for gifting me a pleasant evening after a tiresome day at work. We placed our order and waited for the dishes to arrive.

'No amount of coffee, no amount of crying…' he continued singing. The voice of the singer left me spellbound.

'Adi, will you pay attention to me or should I leave?' Sakshi asked pinching me. I was mentally transported to a different world. I wanted to hear more of his soothing voice. I somehow felt an urge to get to know him better. His way of playing the guitar was soothing to my ears. He had a seductive voice which completely mesmerized me. It was one seductive night!

'Adi, we've met after such a long time and look at you. You have changed so much. Have you forgotten how girls should be treated?' She was getting furious. At that moment, it wouldn't have surprised me if she would have thrown the cutlery at me.

I had landed in Delhi on the same day for an official trip. It was justified on her part to get furious at me as she was feeling ignored. I tried to show her that I was paying attention to her even though my mind was elsewhere. But

8

as we know guys can't beat girls at arguments, especially when the girl is your BFF.

'Yes, I am sorry. Tell me, I am listening to you. It's just that…'

'Oh, don't try to fool me. Why are you paying so much attention to the singer? Have you recently turned gay?' she said in a fit of jealousy.

'I am not paying attention to him. I'm listening to his voice. I am sure there is a lot of pain inside him. And anyway, I was just checking out the interiors of the lounge. Quite nice, no?' I said trying to change the topic.

'Chuck it. Here comes peri peri chicken. Taste it. It's one of the best dishes available here,' she smirked.

'Is it? Do you even understand the meaning of the name? Firstly Mia Bella and now this peri peri. This place seems funny.'

She stared at me and I knew it was time for me to keep quiet. I ate my meal in silence. The peri peri chicken was indeed delicious. We followed up the meal with a few drinks.

'Adi, it feels so good to meet you after almost two years. I so wish that you stayed permanently in Delhi. Then you would have been just a call away whenever I needed you.'

'I am still a call away. Anything for you. Just don't call me too often. It will reflect in your bank statement otherwise,' I laughed.

'I'm not a baniya like you. Thank God you're not my boyfriend,' she replied.

'I was kidding. Okay, where is my surprise? You said that you had something for me. Where is it?' I looked here and there to tease her.

She gave me a naughty smile and looked at the manager, gesturing him to bring something in. I was curious to know what she had planned for the evening. She looked excited and nervous too.

After a few minutes, the manager came back holding a huge cake. As soon as he kept the cake on the table, the same singer whose voice had completely mesmerized me played a mellow song on his guitar. I looked at him and we exchanged smiles.

The cake had a picture of me holding a book in my hand. It was Sakshi's favourite picture of me. She had got the cake custom-made especially for the evening. Her gesture made me feel extremely special. The cake was a chocoholic's dream. Rich, thick, and creamy, with a layer of Oreo cookie crumble in the middle.

'Should I take the honour of cutting it myself?' I smiled looking at my image on the cake.

'Yes please. Kindly go ahead. I want to eat you tonight,' she said giving me a wicked smile.

'Then I better cut the other part of the cake as I don't want to spoil the night,' I laughed.

'You moron. You can never change.' She hugged me as I cut the cake.

I fed the first piece of cake to Sakshi followed by the manager. The cake was then cut into smaller pieces and offered to everyone present at the pub. I took one piece of the cake and went towards the singer sitting on the stage. He was still very engrossed in singing. I went closer to him and offered him a piece of the cake. He sensed affection from me and got up to give me a big hug. His hug made me feel like he was hiding immense pain inside him. I wanted to know what was troubling him but waited for the right time to question.

'I hope you loved the surprise,' Sakshi asked wiping the cake from her mouth.

'You made my day. I feel so special. I will remember this moment forever. I am so lucky to have a friend like you in my life. God has been kind to me.'

I still remember the first day we met. We were too shy to talk then, and look at us now! We've become the best of friends. True friendship is rare these days and I've been lucky to have met and made friends with people whom I can trust blindly. Sakshi was one of them. Our bond was extremely special and unique in its own way. I loved her fun personality which somehow never failed to impress me. She was always there for me whenever I felt blue. The world would definitely be a better place with more people like her.

It was almost 12 am and the pub was supposed to shut down by 1. She introduced me to the manager Anuj, who happened to be her friend. The first few minutes between us were a bit awkward but then I finally decided to break the ice.

'Anuj, can I ask you one thing? Something's been on my mind ever since we came to this place,' I whispered.

'Yes. What's bothering you?' he asked pulling out a chair. 'This guy. The singer. Do you know anything about him?' I continued.

'Not really. But I know that he was a part of one of the most famous college bands in Delhi.'

My sixth sense was right! But why was he here? If he had been a part of one of the most famous bands in Delhi, why was he performing in a restaurant? The more I thought about it, the more I felt he was hiding something and that there was more to him than met the eye.

'Can you introduce me to him?' I requested.

I turned to look at Sakshi, anticipating a long speech. But to my surprise, she too looked interested in knowing who the guy really was.

'Why not? Give me a minute. Let me go talk to him,' said Anuj and started walking towards the singer.

We watched them talking in hushed tones from a distance. Then the guy laid down his guitar near the bar counter and started walking towards us. Sakshi nudged me to lead the introductions.

'Hi, I am Aditya. This is my friend Sakshi. Please take a seat,' I offered.

He took a chair and sat next to us. He looked around but didn't utter a word. Silence filled the air. By then the music had stopped too. We were the only ones left in the pub.

'Anuj told me that you were part of a famous college band. Must have been exciting?'

'No,' he replied.

'Don't worry. We all are friends,' Anuj said trying to make him feel at ease.

'May I know your band name?' Sakshi asked him.

He stared at her for a few seconds. He seemed lost. Though he was physically with us, his mind was elsewhere. Finally, he looked me in the eye and said, 'VAYU'.

I don't know what came over me when he said that name but by then I had made up my mind that I had to ask him everything about the band. Every minute detail. I asked him if he felt comfortable answering my questions.

'I don't mind you asking me about the band even though it will bring back all the memories I'd rather keep hidden away. But I just want to know why it is of interest to you? You had nothing to do with the band.'

I ordered drinks for all of us. Considering the manager was Sakshi's friend, he did not say no even though the pub had shut down by then. It was like a wave of curiosity had engulfed him as well.

'Dude, everyone has a bitter past. We all go through so much in life. We should not cry over past memories but learn from them. The best thing about the worst time of your life is that you get to see the truth behind everyone you've ever cared for. If you think you're okay with sharing your story with us, then please do. We'd love to hear it.'

I tried my best to convince him. Sakshi also did her part by making him understand that we were not being intrusive but were fascinated to know more. After Anuj's repeated requests, he finally gave in.

'Can I have a glass of water?' he asked Anuj.

Anuj went to bring a glass of water for him. By that time, even the bar counter had shut. I had already called for drinks. I was just about to shoot my first question when the guy broke the silence.

'I am Vikrant, the drummer of the band VAYU.'

I looked at him with curiosity. He had a slight smile on his face. His eyes spoke a thousand words.

'We use to be one of the most promising bands on the scene. Rajhans College was proud to have a band like us. 'We had named it VAYU.'

'Interesting. But why are you here? Is this your part-time job? And if you were the drummer, then how were you playing the guitar so flawlessly and singing in such a mesmerizing voice?' I asked.

'You ask too many questions. Relax,' he said taking a sip of the drink in his hand.

I closed my eyes and waited for him to continue. I had no idea what he had gone through and how he had landed in this situation. I had no idea about their band but I was eager to know more. Within a few minutes, he had left everyone engrossed.

'Every person has a story to tell. Some live forever and some die young. Every dream has wings. Some fly forever and some are torn young. Life is so strange. Sometimes it gives you so much that you don't know how to handle it and sometimes it takes away all that it gave you in the same breath. I was caught between two people. They were my

14

best friends in college. But I liked her more than him. Not because she was beautiful but because she was brave enough to face the cruel world on her own and in her own style. She had a carefree attitude but somewhere within her, she cared for everyone she knew.'

'What was her name?' Sakshi couldn't resist asking.

'Anamika. The "A" of VAYU.'

As he recalled his past, I knew I was about to hear the most thrilling story ever...

VAYU—The Wave

Rajhans College, Delhi
30th July, 2012

'Are you Anamika? Miss Malini wants you in the auditorium,' informed the college peon.

'Thanks,' she replied and headed towards the auditorium.

Brought up in Delhi, Anamika had secured admission in Rajhans College for a BCom course through the Extra-curricular Activities (ECA) Quota. She was beautiful, with a lot of style and grace. The red highlights in her hair shone in the sunlight. She had an I-don't-care attitude about her and hated bitching, unlike the other girls in college. She never feared taking risks and could do anything when challenged. She was smoking hot and loved getting tattoos inked on her body. She had got two done so far. One was of a peacock on her lower back and the other was of a butterfly on the left side of her neck. Though she never paid attention to what others thought of her, secretly she wanted to be loved by everyone. She was a firm believer in spirituality.

She always dreamt of being part of a college band and had strived hard to see her dream turn into a reality. She was fond of dancing as well and wanted to be a dancer for the band.

The first semester of college had commenced on 23rd July. Rajhans College was holding auditions for the college band and had shortlisted a few students within the first week. Anamika had high hopes of getting selected. She nervously walked towards the auditorium.

'Hello ma'am, may I come in?' she asked in a low tone.

'Anamika, I've been waiting for you. How are you doing?' said the teacher keeping the files in her hand on the table in front of her. Anamika gave her a warm smile trying to hide her nervousness. Without any more delay, the teacher told her that she had been shortlisted for the band along with two other guys. Her happiness knew no bounds. She screamed out loudly, forgetting she was still in the college premises and that classes were going on.

'Thank you so much. I have no words to say. It was my dream to get shortlisted. I am on cloud nine.'

'Your group still has to clear the final round of auditions. One more group will perform along with you. The best one wins,' she said in a tone of authority.

'My group? Who are the rest of the band members?' Anamika questioned.

'Vikrant and Yuvi. I have informed Yuvi about his selection and he'll be here any moment now. Can you call up Vikrant and ask him by when he will reach?' she said handing her phone to Anamika. It had Vikrant's number displaying on the screen.

Anamika dialled Vikrant's number and after a brief introduction, asked him about his whereabouts. Vikrant told her that he was in the metro and would reach college in an hour.

Vikrant, like Anamika, had got admission in Rajhans College through the ECA Quota. He was well-built and six feet tall. He never combed his hair and liked to wear them spiked in the front. He was smart looking and did not smoke or drink. He was, what we call, a 'one woman' man.

He entered a not-so crowded metro and took a seat. In front of him stood a beautiful girl dressed in a pink salwar-kameez. She had wheatish skin and lustrous black hair that she wore in a ponytail. He gazed at her for a few seconds and looked the other way to avoid embarrassment. As more and more people entered the metro with each passing station, it became difficult for him to see the girl clearly. After some time she stared back at him which made his heart beat even faster than before. It gave him the courage to look at her again. As she cast a glance at him, he stared back at her and their eyes met. It was like the world had come to a standstill. And in that split second of pure bliss, he felt like she was as attracted to him as he was to her. Their mutual attraction became stronger with each passing minute. He imagined a scenario where she would be on his side and he would be in complete ecstasy as he held her close to him. Perhaps on the beach, hearing the sounds of the waves crashing, feeling the cool water beneath their feet. She would then pull his face to her lips as he would pull her body closer to him. All of this raced through his mind as she looked at him for those three and a half seconds. Their mutual gaze made him realize this could be the start of something grand. He had already imagined a lifetime with her when suddenly a woman's voice brought him back to reality.

'Agla station Rajeev Chowk hai. The next station is Rajeev Chowk. Darwaaze baayi aur khulenge. Kripya darwaze se hat kar khade hoye. Doors will open on the left. Please stand clear of the door.'

He looked for her amid the crowd and saw her standing near the door. He looked at her for one final time before the door opened and she exited, disappearing from his eyesight. With every move, she enchanted his heart. He felt like she was looking back at him and that their eyes met for a fleeting second. Before he could continue dreaming about the girl, his station came and he got down from the metro. As he walked towards the exit gate, he thought about the auditions he had given earlier for their college's lead band. Anamika had already told him that he had been shortlisted and he was excited and geared up for the final audition round.

'Hey. I am here,' he announced as he entered the auditorium.

'Vikrant right?' Miss Malini asked.

'Yes.'

'Great to see you. We are proud to have you in our college. You were the best among all of them. Congratulations.'

'Thanks ma'am. I will prove my calibre in the final round,' he said with determination.

'Where is Yuvi? He should have been here by now,' Anamika asked.

'I am here,' Yuvi screamed entering the auditorium.

Yuvi, the lead guitarist and vocalist, was extremely fond of bikes. He was so good looking that any girl could fall in love with him in a second. He had an athletic body, with broad shoulders, bulging biceps, and sensual lips. He had a slight hint of a beard. To most girls' dismay, he was in a committed relationship with a girl he had been seeing since the past four years. He was someone who didn't follow but made rules. He was different from everybody else around him. He wore a piercing near his eyebrow and was never low on energy. He could stay up all night long and still drop her girlfriend to work the next morning. However, he wouldn't mind giving a lift to a sexy girl while returning home. He entered the auditorium wearing a hat and a headband.

'So, who are our opponents? I am sure they can't beat us. At least not me. You guys up for it?' he asked.

Vikrant was thoroughly miffed with his attitude but he disregarded it for the band's sake. They just had a few hours left to practice before their final round audition. All three exchanged quick introductions and started rehearsing aggressively. The opponents too wanted to win the coveted spot anyhow. Both the groups knew that once they were made part of the college band, there was no looking back. They would get popular in no time and be able to make their mark in the world of music.

The rehearsal got over and it was time for the live performance. The judges were sitting in the first row of the auditorium waiting for both the groups to perform. Only volunteers were allowed to enter the auditorium. The decision was completely in the hand of judges. Vikrant, Anamika, and Yuvi walked on stage and gave each other one last look before starting the performance.

'Good evening judges. We hope you like our song.'

> *Jo tujhe jagaaye, neende teri udaaye,*
> *Khwaab hai sachha wahi...*
> *Neendo me jo aaye, jise tu bhul jaaye,*
> *Khwaab who sachha nahi...*

Yuvi played the guitar and started humming the song while Anamika moved her body to the beats of the music. Vikrant too played the drums to perfection. In the two minutes that were given to them, they sang their hearts out. The judges gave them a huge round of applause at the end of the performance.

They bowed in front of the judges and left the stage. They were told to wait outside the auditorium till the other band finished performing. They tried to contain their nervous energy and were confident of securing a win over their competition.

'You think we can make it, guys?' Anamika asked both of them.

'They don't have a choice,' Yuvi answered.

'We have given it our best shot. Now let's just keep our fingers crossed and hope for the best,' Vikrant replied.

They were called inside the auditorium a few minutes later after their opponent's performance ended. Both the bands stood on stage while the judges discussed their respective performances and scribbled something in their notepads. After a few minutes, the judges came on stage to announce the winner. A long silence engulfed the auditorium. Both the bands stared at each other in silence. Their dislike for each other was quite visible through their body language. Anamika shut her eyes and prayed silently to the almighty. Vikrant and Yuvi looked chilled out since they were confident of their win.

'Students, we are so happy to have such fresh talent like you in our college. For us, both teams are winners. However, the rules say that only one team can win. So all three judges have carefully graded your final act taking many factors into consideration and have reached a decision. We request the group who loses to accept the decision with grace. Without wasting any more time, let me announce the winner,' said one of the judges.

'And the winner is…Group A! Vikrant, Yuvi, and Anamika.'

All three of them hugged each other in joy. The three of them had overcome all the odds and finally achieved what they always wanted. They had been able to overcome all their fears. They went on stage to shake hands with the judges. The trio was now the official band of Rajhans College. They decided to hang out in the evening before embarking on their new journey.

'Where should we go? Let's go to some lounge,' Anamika suggested.

'I don't drink. Sorry,' Vikrant said in low tone.

'Oh, shut up Vikrant. Stop being a kid. Anamika, let's go to the (V) Spot Café & Bar in Saket,' said an excited Yuvi.

'Don't worry. I will give you company,' said Vikrant.

'Oh, great. So what will you do there? Eat green salad and drink apple juice?' Yuvi teased him and all three of them erupted in laughter.

'Ok guys. See you in the evening,' said Anamika bidding them goodbye.

While Vikrant and Anamika took the Metro, Yuvi decided to come by his car. All three agreed to meet at the Hauz Khaz metro station. Once they reached the station, Vikrant and Anamika got into Yuvi's car and Yuvi raced the car towards Saket.

'I just love to go on a long drive. We used to go on the Yamuna Expressway. I mean me and my boyfriend,' Anamika exclaimed.

'Where is he now?' Vikrant asked.

'I dumped him some time back. He was a coward. Bloody dumbass,' Anamika said in apparent disgust. 'I suppose he was a nerd. How else would he have let such a sexy girl like you go away so easily?' Yuvi replied gazing at her.

'Shut up. So what about you? Dating anyone?' she asked.

'I am committed. Her name is Kashish.'

'Aye haye. Kya baat hai,' Anamika teased him.

They tried to locate the bar and finally found it in one of the by-lanes behind Select Citywalk mall. It was Tuesday evening and the bar was almost vacant. The décor was eye-catching. There was also an LED screen that kept flashing funny one-liners. After taking their seats, they ordered cocktails and mocktails along with a few starters.

'Anamika, did you always want to be part of a music band?' Yuvi asked in a casual tone.

'Yes. I would always fight with my parents about it. I hardly cared about people who tried to pull me down. I knew I was the best and was not afraid of saying so. But dancing is my passion. I have even taken professional dance classes to sharpen my skills. I want to see myself at the top. I fear losing.'

'You fear losing? What does that mean? Be a sport. We cannot win every time,' Vikrant added.

'I know. But my fear is not only for competitions. I fear ragging too. It's the first week of college and I'm sure the seniors are out to get us,' she said sipping her drink.

'You should take leave then. Don't come to college for one week,' Yuvi laughed.

'Chuck it. I will find some other way of avoiding them. So tell me, what's your dream?' she asked Yuvi.

'To be a rock star. I always dream of people shouting my name as I entertain them with my music. It was my dream to be a lead vocalist for my college and today I have achieved it,' Yuvi exclaimed.

'But don't forget that we still have a long way to go. We should be a name to reckon with in all of Delhi University,' stated Vikrant.

Anamika and Yuvi got up from their seat to where Vikrant was sitting. Before Vikrant could interpret what was happening, they started punching him lightly in his stomach.

'Why are you always so serious? Don't you know how to enjoy a joke?' they laughed. One solid group was in the making. Though it had been only a couple of days since they met, their friendship seemed old. They were very comfortable in each other's company. Most friendships only last for a particular phase of our lives. For a friendship to last forever, there has to be bonding in the group. There must be a connection that surpasses time and space constraints. They had those commonalities between them. Anamika was a carefree girl who could do anything to overcome her fear, who cared for the band, and who found utmost joy and comfort in the group. Vikrant was a serious guy who believed in perfection. Yuvi, though born into a rich family, was very grounded and enjoyed Anamika and Vikrant's company a great deal.

After having relaxed at the bar for over two hours, they gave hi-fives to each other and left the place. On impulse, they decided to go for a long drive in Yuvi's car.

🏸

'Have you thought of a name for our band?' Yuvi asked.

'Are we allowed to keep the name ourselves?' Anamika questioned.

'Who cares? I just want a name for our band so that we get an identity of our own,' Yuvi said.

'Agnee?' Anamika suggested.

'No yaar. There's already a famous band by that name. We can't use it. We need to have a unique name. One that has never been used by anyone before. Our name should not only have a deeper meaning to it, it should also be symbolic of our hidden passion for music,' said Yuvi stepping on the accelerator to take the car to a speed of 100 km/hr. The cool breeze ruffled Vikrant's hair caressingly and as he tried to push back the mop of hair from his forehead, the name struck him!

'VAYU!' Vikrant shouted.

All of a sudden, Yuvi applied the brakes and the car came to a screeching halt on the highway.

'Does it mean wind?' Anamika questioned.

'No. I mean yes.' Vikrant stammered.

'What does it mean exactly?' Yuvi asked. He had taken a liking to that name as well, just like the other two band members.

'It means us. We, the band.'

'What are you saying?' Anamika questioned again.

'VAYU means wind. We will blow like the mighty winds in all Delhi. But VAYU also means we the group. V for Vikrant, A for Anamika, and Y for Yuvi,' Vikrant said nervously.

'You are a champ man. What a name. Excellent. We, the VAYU,' Yuvi screamed in joy.

'But what does U mean. We don't have anyone by that name,' Anamika added.

'U stands for Us—we make the group, don't we?' Vikrant added.

All three got out of the car and hugged each other. Words had taken a backseat. It is not always long conversations that convey the deepest feelings. Sometimes, such conversations seem redundant. All of them had a common dream. To make their band successful. To be on top. They had climbed the first step of success and there was no looking back from here onwards. As soon as they realized that they were in the middle of the highway, they got into the car and sped away. Yuvi dropped Anamika and Vikrant at Rajiv Chowk metro station. Vikrant and Anamika took two different lines—Vikrant took the blue line metro while Anamika the yellow line metro.

While waiting for the metro, Vikrant was reliving that evening with the other band mates. He was looking forward to performing with them. His thoughts were shattered when he saw the same girl he had encountered a few days ago in the metro standing only a few feet away from him. His heart skipped a beat. He thought of walking up to her and exchanging a few words, but something in him stopped him from taking a step forward. Her book fell down and she bent to pick it up. A few strands of hair partially covered her face, blocking his view. She adjusted her dupatta and looked around to ensure no one was watching her.

Vikrant's heart was in his mouth and he turned his back to her immediately to escape being seen by her. A metro entered the platform. After a few seconds, he again turned to see if she had entered the metro. She was nowhere to be seen on the platform, so he assumed she had got in. He too got inside immediately before the gates could shut. He somehow squeezed himself in, but the metro was too crowded and he couldn't see the girl anywhere. All his senses suddenly had a heightened intensity. The colours seemed brighter, the sounds seemed louder, and the smells seemed more powerful. When your love is in front of your eyes, you don't need any one around you to keep you company. But when your love is away, you spend all your time thinking of each other. When you are truly in love, nature has its own way of acknowledging it. Maybe a leaf flutters or a light breeze blows past you. When would nature give him a sign? Was his emotion love? Every beginning however always has a sequel.

Wo nazar kaha se lau jo tumhe bhula de,
Wo dawa kaha se lau jo is dard ko mita de.
Milna likha hota hai takdiro me,
Par wo takdir hi kaha se lau jo hum dono ko mila de!

From 'It's Complicated' to 'In a Relationship'

Rajhans College, Delhi
4th August, 2012

'Sanaya, things are just not working between us. I think we should take a break,' said Anurag.

'What's wrong with you? You say the same thing every day. Has it become a daily routine for you now?' Sanaya shouted back.

'That's what I am saying. Let's stop it. There is no point in stretching this anymore because we're only heading towards a dead end. Anyway, you seem quite happy with that guy from your batch. The one with curly hair,' he said with a hint of sarcasm.

'Are you insane? I mean how can you even think I like him? You think I am a bloody bitch? I am not a slut who sleeps around with everyone. Please yaar. You are impossible.'

The conversation turned ugly when Anurag became aggressive and violent.

'Everyone was right. You are a jerk. All my friends were against our relationship but still I trusted you,' she cried.

'Oh, so you mean I forced you to become my girlfriend? You hypocrite. Just buzz off,' Anurag said pushing Sanaya away.

A spoiled brat, Anurag was the president of the Student's Union of Rajhans College. Other students in the college would say 'Kuch bhi karneka lekin Anurag ka ego hurt nahi karneka.' He hated going to the gym and even though he was not very tall, he had an excellent dressing sense. He never wore anything apart from the latest brands. Be it Puma shoes or a Rolex watch. Despite his image, he was popular among the girls because he never let them pay the bills during outings and would take them for long drives in his Audi. The other boys in college kept their distance from him out of fear. Only his closest friends knew that he was not a bad person at heart but was just self-centred.

Sanaya on the other hand was a very studious girl who loved reading novels during her spare time. She didn't like going to parties. Small surprises were enough to bring a sparkle in her eyes. She was quite broad-minded when it came to relationships and she loved to be with her friends. She was a bubbly, full of life girl who could carry western as well as Indian outfits with equal style. Her slim body and wheatish skin made her the perfect girl next door. Though a lot of guys proposed to her before Anurag, she could never really get herself to say yes to any one of them. Then she started seeing Anurag in her first year. Slowly she began to realize that Anurag was not her type of guy. He used to flirt around openly with other girls, roam on the streets at midnight, and loved staying overnight at his friends' houses after parties. Things started getting sour as the days passed, but still Sanaya tried hard to hold on to their relationship. However, Anurag had taken the decision. Some relationships have to end to make way for a new beginning.

'What's the matter, Anurag? I gave you everything you wanted. I came with you for an overnight stay too. And look at your behaviour towards me. Is this the right way to behave?' she asked seeking justification for the sudden breakup.

'Don't piss me off anymore, you bitch. Go away, or else bear the consequences. Do you want to create a scene in front of everyone?' Anurag said looking around at the students passing by.

'Oh really? What do you want to prove? That I sleep around with guys. You want to show to your friends that you are a casanova who flirt around and sleeps with girls? Or you're trying to be authoritative with me? For you I have just one word. Tharki. I wish I could kick your balls right now so that you learn a lesson.'

Anurag didn't even blink an eye. He was listening to all the allegations she was making at him. He didn't utter a single word. This continued for a few more minutes. Some students stood in a corner watching the entire act. It certainly hurt his ego. What followed was the reaction to Sanaya's action that left everybody shocked.

Bangg!! He slapped her hard and she fell to the ground. He then left the college premises, leaving her to fend for herself. She wondered what her fault was. A few students picked her up from the ground and dusted off the dirt from her dress. They tried to console her but she left the college premises with tears in her eyes. Anurag had not only slapped her but also her love, trust, and soul. When two people are intimate with each other, that is the highest level that a relationship can reach. Whether a breakup is cordial or not, one thing is for sure that it makes a monumental difference in the lives of the people involved.

It was a lonely night for her. Feeling sad and depressed, she messaged him though she knew it was useless waiting for a reply.

You came to me like a wave that goes away in a fraction of a second. You change your moods like the change of seasons. Just like an ocean will never run out of water and the sky won't ever change its colour to another colour, I don't want to run out of your love. Like peanut butter and jelly, I want us to be together. But it seems like you had other plans for yourself. At least you could have asked me once what I needed or what my expectations were. I want you to be happy and I know there is a guy for me out there who will keep me happy too. I won't cry over you. Certainly not after what you did in the college premises. I am leaving and there's no turning back.

As expected, Anurag didn't reply.

The feeling of being in love is so intense that it feels like it will last forever. And when the other person doesn't feel the same way about us, our dreams are shattered. We can't believe that this sacred relationship has been betrayed. You may have been sure that you had the same wavelength and that you understood each other. But the truth is that you have been walking parallel to each other and end up taking different paths somewhere during your journey.

Sanaya decided it was time for her to move on. She understood she needed to live for the present. She did not want to get back with Anurag, especially after he insulted her in front of everyone. She knew dating him was a mistake. But somewhere she still loved him and would get hurt when Anurag would flirt with other girls from her batch in front of her very eyes! His eyes were now set on the most popular girl from the first year batch. Every year, there is one girl on whom every guy tries his luck. Anurag was hell bent on making this particular girl go out with him at all costs. Her name was…

Anamika!

Anurag logged into his Facebook account and searched for Anamika's profile. Luckily her profile was not completely locked and he was able to check out a few of her pictures. From her snaps he could gather that she was fond of beer and pizzas. Anurag wasn't looking for a serious relationship. All he wanted was a girlfriend to kill time with. He settled on Anamika because he had heard she was open-minded unlike Sanaya and loved partying. She was a perfect catch for him.

It was Friendship Day. Anurag went to college looking for Anamika. Though it was a Sunday, many students were in college to celebrate the day. He spotted Anamika sitting in the college lawns with Vikrant and Yuvi. Even though she was with two guys at the time, Anurag was not at all afraid to approach her. He was dressed in a Polo T-shirt because she had 'liked' the Polo T-shirts fan page on Facebook.

'Anamika,' he called out to her.

Anamika was busy chatting with her band mates when she heard Anurag's voice shout her name. She looked up to see Anurag standing in front of her. She vaguely knew about him as he was the president of the Student's Union and owned an Audi.

'Hi. I am Anamika. First-year student and a part of our college band. How do you know me?' she asked in a friendly tone.

'Oh come on…half of the college is your fan and you're asking me how do I know you? That's strange, pretty lady. By the way, Happy Friendship Day!' he said handing her a yellow rose.

'Thank you so much,' Anamika said with a blush as she accepted the yellow rose from Anurag.

She signalled Vikrant and Yuvi to go for their classes and leave them alone.

'I saw a few dance videos of you on Facebook and trust me, you are a fabulous dancer,' Anurag said praising her. Anamika thanked him and they continued walking. Anamika loved it when someone praised her.

Soon they reached 'Lover's Point' aka the college canteen.

'Do you know why this place is called Lover's Point?' Anurag asked.

'No.'

'Generally when we hear the name, we visualize a cozy corner or a garden where couples spend time away from the worries of the world. But this place got its name because it is believed that SRK proposed to Gauri right here and since then it's been called LP.'

'You must be kidding,' she laughed.

'I am dead serious, girl,' said Anurag patting her on the shoulder. Anamika showed no objection, much to his joy. She knew where it was heading and she was okay with it.

After spending some time together, they decided to part for the day, but not before exchanging their numbers. Anamika went to her class where Vikrant and Yuvi were waiting for her curiously as they wanted to know what was going on between them. She told them everything which confused them even further. Their confusion was not regarding Anurag but regarding Anamika's behaviour. They could not believe she was giving in to his wishes since they had heard he had a bad reputation. She said that she had made friends with him because she wanted to save herself from ragging.

'Guys, I told you that I have this phobia and I can't overcome it. I think Anurag's company will save me from ragging. I don't want to be a victim, especially when I know so many people are dying to rag me. I better stay with

Anurag than fall prey to those in a mood to rag and feast on me.'

Ever since a young age, she was told horrible stories about ragging which instilled that fear in her. The media had made it equally worse. She had recently seen an episode of ragging on the reality show *Gumrah* which reinforced her fear. Yuvi and Vikrant couldn't understand why she feared ragging so much, but that's how Anamika was. She was willing to do anything to avoid ragging and Anurag was her safety net. Strange was the start of their friendship. Neither Anurag was serious about dating her nor was she. They both had selfish motives behind their actions.

Anurag had called Anamika at the Q'BA lounge & bar which was situated at Connaught place. She had a brief idea of what was coming her way. A yellow rose was going to be replaced by a red one symbolizing his love for her.

Anamika sent a WhatsApp message to Anurag the next morning, *'Where are you? Meet me at Rajiv Chowk. I am coming directly from my rehearsal.'*

Anurag replied soon after, *'I am near AIIMS. Should I come to pick you up? I don't mind spending a few litres of petrol just to make sure you reach safely. After all, your safety is of prime concern to me,'* he replied in a flirty tone.

'No need. I'll be there in some time. Till then, you can practice flirting with someone else,' she replied with a winking smiley.

'*That's just for you, my sweetheart.*'

Anamika smiled and kept the phone back in her pocket. She took the metro to Rajeev Chowk and all along the way, she kept thinking about Anurag. She had made up her mind that the latest developments in her personal life won't affect the band adversely. Though Vikrant and Yuvi had doubts about her seeing Anurag, she had been able to convince them that it won't harm the performance and the group bonding in any way. She was nervous about meeting Anurag as she didn't trust him and feared landing in a mess. However, she had to take the risk with him to escape ragging. As soon as she reached Connaught Place, she saw Anurag waiting outside his car in the parking spot outside Q'BA bar and restaurant.

After greeting her, he escorted her to the restaurant. They entered the lounge area which had a swanky bar in the middle and was decorated with beautiful lamps all around. They took their seats and Anurag called for the menu card even though he had decided what he wanted to order.

'Beer and one smoked chicken pizza,' he told the waiter.

'Hey, I love smoked chicken pizza. How did you know?' Anamika exclaimed.

'Just took a wild guess,' Anurag replied with a smug expression. Things were going according to plan.

Anamika was looking dazzling in black shorts and a tank top. She flaunted her tattoos on purpose.

'After visiting the same old eateries over and over again, this place is like a breath of fresh air,' said Anurag.

'I completely agree with you. All the other places are so loud,' Anamika added.

'That's the reason I brought you here. So I could listen to your sexy, mesmerizing voice,' Anurag said taking her hand in his. Anamika simply smiled and looked away shyly.

The warmth of his touch flowed from his hand to hers. It felt like a promise of togetherness. With every passing minute, his grip on her hand became stronger. He gently kissed her on the palm like a thorough gentleman. After they were done with drinks and food, Anurag dropped Anamika home. After she got down from the car, he gave her a slight peck on her cheek. Anamika didn't object to it. She was expecting him to say those three golden words. But he didn't and zoomed away in his car.

After reaching home, Anurag sent her a text message.

When I first interacted with you, you were sweet and genuine. It felt like a string connected me directly to your heart. There is something strong taking place between us and instead of letting it pass, we should act upon it. Now sleep tight and get ready as tomorrow will be special for you.

Rabb kare tu sada hasdi rahe,
Koi dukh tere nere vi na aaye.
Hor ki dua maanga rab to,
Tenu sadi vi umar lag jaye!!

Anurag kept his phone on silent mode after sending the text. He knew he had hit the right chord and in the process of doing this, he had actually developed a soft corner for Anamika! A relationship that was meant to be mere fun was heading in a completely new direction. However, he was unaware of Anamika's real intentions.

Anamika didn't reply back.

Rajhans College, Delhi
6th August, 2012

Anamika was one of the first students to reach college the next day. Though it was Anurag who had called her so early, she couldn't see him anywhere nor was he picking up calls. Anamika was surprised by this strange behaviour of his and asked a few students hovering around if they had seen Anurag, but they had no clue. Finally she gave up her search and thought of waiting for her band mates in the canteen. She was extremely hungry because she had skipped breakfast in a rush. She ordered chole bhature and again called Anurag, but his phone was not reachable.

After a few minutes, the canteen boy brought her order. She was annoyed to find the steel bowl containing the chole covered with foil. She opened the covering and found one paper inside it.

'Anamika, today you can only eat Anurag's love for breakfast. He is waiting for you in the library.'

This brought a big smile to her face. The canteen boy was looking at her with a quizzical expression. Anamika understood why Anurag had avoided meeting her that morning. He wanted to surprise her with a note.

Anurag had already done 'setting' with the canteen boys and considering he was the president of the Student's Union, they had to honour his wishes. Another canteen boy came and handed her a bouquet of red roses with another note:

You might be annoyed at me, thinking I am doing time pass with you. But I really like you. Maybe it's love… I don't know yet. But what I do know is that I missed you a lot last night. I have really started caring for you…my love, my baby, my sweetheart. There is something about you which makes me think of you every minute. I've always felt my life is a puzzle, but there was a piece missing. That missing piece is you. You complete me. I never thought love will happen so soon to me. Your presence sends shivers down my spine. Being with you has made me realize that you are the one for me. Someone for whom I can give my life. I want to give you all the happiness you want. All I want is your trust. You will hear students saying all kinds of stuff about me, but your trust will keep this relationship alive. I am waiting in the library for you. Anamika, I love you. I need you. I am all yours. Can you be mine?

She walked towards the library with the bunch of flowers in her hands. She loved the way Anurag surprised her with little gifts. She thought of messaging Vikrant and Yuvi about the sudden change of plans, but then decided to tell them personally.

She didn't want to do anything special for him like other girls usually do for their boyfriends, not because she had a motive behind the relationship, but because she was aware that most of the guys were happy enough just having a girlfriend by their side. Anurag was definitely one of them. She reached the library but saw no one. She could just hear the tapping of feet in one corner. This made her heart beat faster.

Anurag could sense Anamika coming closer to her. Both couldn't see each other due to the rack of books that separated them, but there was obvious sexual tension in the air. The library was completely empty and there was pin drop silence. Anurag was taking full advantage of that. Anurag slowly took a few steps in her direction. He went closer to her. Anamika stood still when she saw him approaching from a distance. When they were merely a step apart, Anurag took her hands in his as she looked into his eyes. Suddenly, Anamika hugged him tightly and shut her eyes. Anurag held her by her waist and stroked her hair. For a few moments, both stood in perfect silence.

'I love you, Anamika. Don't take this the wrong way,' Anurag said breaking the silence.

'I love you too,' Anamika added.

'Do you really love me?' she added as an afterthought.

'Anamika, I am yours. I may have a bad image in college, but this time I am serious about you. I am not saying this because I want to show you off as my girlfriend. I will prove it to you that I really care for you. Whenever you are close to me, I feel a burning desire in me that I had never felt before. You know I was in a relationship before, but there was no compatibility between us. Even the passion was missing. What I feel for you this moment is something special. Trust me,' he said.

He gave her a peck on the cheek and wrapped her in his arms while caressing her back. He kissed her neck and gave her a passionate smooch on her lips.

'Someone might come. This place is not safe,' Anamika whispered while Anurag tried to slip his hand in her top.

'Don't worry. I am keeping an eye. Let me feel your love. Let me feel this burning desire,' he muttered as she moaned passionately.

Anamika gave him a naughty smile and they were lost in complete ecstasy, forgetting that they were in the college library. Wat it lust or love…neither knew at that point. Anurag's feelings for Anamika were getting stronger with each passing minute where he tried to feel her body. But Anamika didn't allow him to cross his limits either. She didn't want to set any false expectations.

Anamika informed Vikrant and Yuvi that she had accepted Anurag's proposal and was now in a relationship with him. She left in a hurry because she had a date with Anurag. She promised to introduce Vikrant and Yuvi to him the next day.

As she walked away, Vikrant kept thinking how she made it look so easy. Or was she putting on an act? It is never so simple that a girl accepts a proposal to just save herself from getting ragged.

'Is she doing the right thing? I mean she is a girl. What about her image?' Vikrant asked Yuvi.

'Oh, cut the crap. What girl and all? She knows what she is doing. Even you know what our seniors would have done had she said no to him. And what's the big deal? That's her personal life. That's her decision. It's simple. I just don't want our band to get affected by all these things,' Yuvi answered.

Vikrant remembered the promise Anamika had made to him and convinced himself that she was not wrong. Even though Vikrant and Yuvi barely knew anything about Anamika, they knew that she wasn't going to let anyone use her for his own personal gains. Moreover, for a girl like her, it was always difficult to get away from people's attention.

Do Not Disturb

10th August, 2012

It's said that when one wants to live life to the fullest, one should go to college and when one wants to attain knowledge, one should go to the library. What's there in college apart from sipping a few glasses of beer and roaming around with beautiful girls? Nothing at all!

Members of VAYU were living a life they had always dreamed of. Vikrant was delighted to be in the company of Yuvi and Anamika during college, but his nights were reserved for dreams of the girl whom he had seen a couple of times in the metro. Anamika had overcome her initial phobia and was now in a steady relationship with Anurag after promising her group that her love life won't affect the band in any way. Yuvi had his girlfriend Kashish to keep him company. Sanaya too had decided to move on after coming to know that Anurag was now dating Anamika.

Yuvi and Kashish had decided to spend a day out together as they had completed four years of their relationship.

Another reason why they wanted to spend time together was that Yuvi would get extremely busy in rehearsals for the band's live performance that was scheduled for Saturday, 18th August. Yuvi had asked Vikrant to tag along with them too. Both of them left from college early that day.

'Where are you guys meeting? I mean, where is she waiting for you?' Vikrant asked as he took his seat in the car.

'Khan Market,' Yuvi said adjusting the mirror.

'Any special plans?'

'Nothing really. We will have lunch and then a movie or probably go back to my home. Let's see,' Yuvi replied.

Anamika called Vikrant to inform him that their practice for the show was scheduled to commence from the next day onwards. Vikrant informed Yuvi about it.

'I hope our show goes well,' said Vikrant.

'It will. Just that Anamika needs to get her act together. I don't know… There's something that's changed about her ever since she started going out with that Anurag guy. Sometimes I hate her for it as I think her relationship will spoil everything we've planned. I get this weird feeling every time I see her with him. Maybe all the drugs I've been on are causing the hallucinations," Yuvi said.

'Kya bole ja rahe ho yaar. Leave it. A few minutes ago you were saying she is not wrong and that she has promised us nothing will happen. So why are you doubting her now?' Vikrant asked.

'Have you met Sanaya?' Yuvi asked.

'No, why? Who is she?'

'She was Anurag's girlfriend. She had come to me to ask what was brewing between Anurag and Anamika. I told her all that I knew but I felt she was upset at what I told her. Either she still loves Anurag or she hates Anamika.'

'Did she ask you this casually?' Vikrant questioned.

'Casually dude. She just came over to me in the canteen. I entertained her questions because she was looking upset. We chatted over a cup of coffee and she told me all about herself,' Yuvi said.

'What the hell! Where was I that time? I could have given you guys company. I could have been the shoulder she cried on,' Vikrant laughed.

'Why not? But you were fucking sleeping at that time… dreaming about that metro girl of yours,' Yuvi added.

They reached Khan Market and Yuvi messaged Kashish telling her that he had reached. He got a message from her saying she would reach in a few minutes.

Kashish was a very sweet and down-to-earth girl. She was someone you could take home to meet your parents. She had dimples to die for and glowing skin that could get her commercial ads for face creams. Her smile could lighten up the whole room. She felt uneasy in the company of strangers but would completely let loose in front of her loved ones. The best quality in her was that she knew exactly how to handle Yuvi which was no child's play. Kashish and Yuvi were a perfect match for each other as they complimented each other beautifully. That's probably why Yuvi had mixed feelings for Anamika since she was the extreme opposite of Kashish. Kashish was not a girl who you could let your imagination run wild every night. She was more the sort of girl you could watch for hours without getting tired.

'Kashish, this is Vikrant and Vikrant this is…'

'Chill. There is no need to be formal,' said Vikrant abruptly stopping Yuvi.

'Cool. Let's go to the Big Chill restaurant,' suggested Yuvi.

'No. Please let's go to OTB,' Kashish sweetly requested.

Yuvi had no option but to agree to her request. After all, it was the supreme court's suggestion. There was no way he could say no to her. Finally, they made their way to Out of the Box restaurant. The ambience was vibrant and there was live music being played. They ordered a hookah with chilled beer. Kashish wasn't a drinker but she never stopped Yuvi from drinking or even smoking weed. She had learnt to accept Yuvi as he was. And four years was a long time to be in a relationship. It certainly called for a celebration.

'Cheers on completing four years. God bless you Yuvi and Kashish. May you have a hundred years of togetherness,' Vikrant said raising a glass to the couple.

It was their day. They hugged each other and Kashish asked Yuvi for her gift.

Yuvi got up and went towards the stage. He took the mike and started singing for her,

'To my love, my sweetheart, and my adorable wife. Though we are not married, we share the same emotions that husbands and wives do. This is a small token of my love for you today to mark the success of our very passionate, successful, and lively relationship.'

Dil ko, tumse pyaar hua,
Pehli baar hua, tumse pyaar hua…
Mein bhi aashiq yaar hua, pehli baar hua,
Tumse pyaar hua!!

Kashish had tears in her eyes. Tears of joy. Tears of happiness. Even Vikrant got teary-eyed. But they were tears of surprise. He was completely unaware of Yuvi's romantic side. There was obviously more to Yuvi than what met the eye. Kashish and Yuvi hugged each other tightly, their hug symbolic of their passion, love, and care for each other.

If you don't understand your companion's silence, you won't understand their words. If you don't understand their pain, you won't understand their tears. If you don't understand their smiles, you won't understand their joy. True love is strong and enduring. But how do we know our love is true and our companion is not fooling around with us? How do we know it's not mere infatuation? How do we know that our relationship has the power to last? The truth is that these questions can be answered only with experience. It may take a few bad relationships to figure out who is truly made for you. Yuvi and Kashish had found that enduring love in each other.

After having lunch together, Vikrant left giving Yuvi and Kashish sometime to spend with each other on their anniversary.

'So Kashish, how does it feel after spending four precious years with me?' Yuvi asked.

'You want to hear the truth?'

'Yes, of course,' he added.

'I never thought that you would love me so much and treat me as your wife even though we aren't married. You know what? Sometimes, I really feel as if we are married. I am seriously lucky to have you in my life and I want you to be very successful in your music career. You say that I am your lucky charm, but it's all your hard work and your parent's blessings that has got you where you are today. But you still have a long way to go. Make us proud, Yuvi. Make me jealous with girls swooning over you, asking for your autograph. But cherish these present moments as they won't last forever. Even if I die before you, then somewhere from the sky I will watch your performances. I will always be with you. You are my best friend, my one true love, my one and only. I love you more today than I did yesterday, and I'll love you more tomorrow than I do today. I promise I won't be a strict wife. Yuvi, never leave me.'

Her speech left him speechless. Kashish loved him more than he could even imagine. His love was the only thing that made her life worth living. In the last four years, she had lived a different life altogether.

'What about you, Yuvi?' she asked holding his hand tightly and resting her head on his shoulders.

'I just want to say that you complete me. I thought that I would never find a love that is as strong as ours. But now that we've found each other I know that you are the girl I want to spend the rest of my life with, the girl I want to marry, the girl I want to have babies with, and the girl I want to grow old with,' Yuvi said kissing her on her forehead and taking her in his arms.

Their bond was unbreakable. No couple could have loved each other as passionately as them. Despite so many girls who wanted Yuvi in their life, he was dedicated to Kashish. The same held true for her as well. They drove to Lodhi Garden on Kashish's wish.

Lodhi Garden, located on Lodhi road, is one of the most famous parks in Delhi. If you can't find a place to romance, you can land up at this place without any hassles. Kashish wanted to take a walk in the lush green gardens with Yuvi.

'What are we going to do in a garden?' Yuvi said confused.

'Romance each other. I have made something for you,' said Kashish and kissed him on the cheek.

All Yuvi could do was give her a slight smile and follow her orders. They entered the garden and walked alongside each other.

'How can you manage to look so beautiful all the time?' he teased her.

'It's your love for me which makes you feel I'm beautiful,' she responded holding him tightly and leaning on him.

'You should have been a writer. You speak so poetically,' he smiled.

'For now I am fine being your girlfriend. But if you insist, I can pen down a few songs for you,' she laughed.

From the day they'd met, God had made them grow closer to each other. Their past pain had vanished and their tears washed away.

Yuvi took her in his arms and started feeling her up.

'What are you doing Yuvi?'

'Exploring your body. Do you have any problem with that? Don't worry, no one is watching us. Wasn't it your idea to come here and romance?'

'Achha. Was it really my idea? When did I say that I was going to put my hands inside your T-shirt the way you are doing now?'

'Did I stop you from doing it?' Yuvi winked.

'Shut up. Now sit quietly and relax. I have brought something for you,' she said and took out something from her purse.

'What's this?' he asked with curiousity.

'Your favourite parathas. I made them for you this morning before leaving from home,' she said pulling his cheeks.

When you are with your love, you have the strength to conquer the world. Yuvi felt the same strength within him. He kept his head on her lap while Kashish fed him the parathas she had made especially for him. In between munches, he bit her fingers a few times just to tease her.

Sometimes he bent her head and kissed her on her forehead. Yuvi kept his head on Kashish's lap while she stroked his hair gently. It's said that people change themselves when they are in love. Yuvi didn't change himself or his feelings. He was still the same guy who shed tears after watching a romantic movie, who preferred weed over a smoke or a hookah, who abused a football player if he missed out on a goal, and who enjoyed playing his guitar or singing even when he was alone. The only time he'd feel satisfied was when he would be in the company of Kashish. They lay on the grass and just watched each other without uttering a word. When it got dark, they decided to leave.

'Where are we going now? Are you dropping me home?' Kashish asked.

'Not so early. You will go home tomorrow morning. There is no one at my place and you are keeping me company tonight,' Yuvi smiled.

'Are you nuts? I can't do that. I have not even informed my parents about my whereabouts. They will kill me,' she said nervously getting into the car.

'Call them now and inform them. Till then, let me get some food packed for us,' said Yuvi heading to a nearby restaurant.

Kashish anxiously called her parents and informed them that she was going to stay with her friends in Janakpuri for the night. After a lot of convincing, her parents finally agreed. She let out a sigh a relief. Yuvi returned with a packet in his hand. Handing her the packet, he took to the drivers' seat and sped off towards his home.

'So what did you tell your parents?' he asked.

'Did you leave me with a choice? I just told them that I was going to stay in Janakpuri with my friend,' she added.

'Kya baat hai. So your Janakpuri friend is going to get wild with you tonight,' he said grabbing her and kissing her passionately.

Kashish responded with the same urgency and wished that their relationship lasts forever. Even after four years of dating, they behaved like love struck teenagers in each other's company who couldn't get enough of each other.

After they reached his apartment, Kashish rested herself on the sofa while Yuvi went to freshen up. Once done, he rolled up some marijuana he was hiding in his jeans pocket, brought it near his lips, and took a puff. He had a habit of smoking marijuana before getting intimate with Kashish. That's the reason he would get rough and extremely wild during their love making sessions. The drug brought out a completely new side to him.

'Come on, how much time are you taking? You want to waste the night?' Kashish winked.

'Sweetheart, it's not a cigarette. It's marijuana, for Christ's sake! It sends me straight to heaven,' he added taking another sniff.

'Let me also try it.'

'You just relax, darling. This is not for girls. I will play your favourite music tonight. What should I play? Milkshake or chocolate candy?'

'Shut up, you dog and let's go inside. I can't wait anymore.'

'You get turned on so easily. I like it. Makes you look sexy,' he said. He was clearly not in his senses.

He told her to go inside and wait for him wearing the costume that he had brought for her. He kept taking one drag after another. He felt everything spinning around him. He got off the chair and moved towards the bedroom where Kashish was waiting for him.

'Are you ready for it?' he asked her and knocked on the bedroom door where she was waiting for him.

'Come in. The door is open. Take me for a ride,' she said in excitement.

Yuvi slowly opened the door and found Kashish sitting on the bed.

'Your nurse is ready, doctor,' she winked biting her lower lip.

He took one look at her in the dress he had brought for her and exclaimed, 'Oh Jesus! You look like a bombshell.'

It was a short white top that could hardly contain her big bosom. The red micro mini skirt showed off her perfectly shaped thighs. Her hair were wet and a few drops of water rolled down her neck, making her look sultry. That's exactly what Yuvi wanted. He walked closer to her, which made his heart beat faster. His desires were at their peak due to the drugs he had consumed a few minutes ago. He wanted to eat her alive.

'You look better without clothes, darling,' he said pulling down her skirt.

'Do I? Come here, you naughty little thing,' she moaned trying to unbuckle his belt but he stopped her.

'Ssssh. It's my turn. Relax.'

He lifted her in his arms and gently placed her on the bed.

'Come here you…'

'Shut up, you bitch! I am going to give you the ultimate pleasure today. Just enjoy the ride, baby,' he said taking out an apple from the drawer next to the bed.

It was not a regular apple! It was OhMiBod, a music-driven vibrator! It translated an electronic music output into vibrations.

'There's your music player,' he said with a naughty smile.

'Get on me now,' she moaned taking off her top.

Yuvi moved closer to her with the vibrator in his hand and laid down beside her.

He brought his mouth to her belly and kissed it.

'How do you feel?' he asked.

'So good, baby. I need you inside me now,' she moaned in pleasure.

'Hold on. I will take you to a different world. The world of imagination, the world of romance, and the world of love.'

Their lips came closer. He rubbed her thighs and caressed her back.

'Why do you have to always kiss with closed eyes? Today you won't close them,' he ordered.

'I find it weird to keep them open,' she answered.

'Open them. It's my order,' he said slapping her back and touching her lips with his fingers the next moment. The drug had aroused his carnal instincts and he wanted to touch every part of her body.

He trembled as her breath tickled his ears. She kissed him on the ear and whispered 'I love you'. The flame of passion, desire, and love took control over them and as he touched her bare skin, she moaned wildly. When she could take it no more, he put the vibrator to work. That was the final touch! It made her go weak in the knees. So weak that she could hardly speak. He crawled seductively between her legs and their bodies met for the ultimate union. Their bed sheet was almost in tatters by the end of their love making session. She was shivering by the end of it.

'That was tiring but so good,' she moaned covering her body with the tattered sheet.

'I love you so much,' he said kissing her on the forehead.

'Do you realize that you are a completely different man after you consume drugs? You forget who am I and who you are. You are so rough and hard,' she teased him.

He didn't utter a word but just took her in his arms and hugged her tightly. Like a kid, she rested her head on his chest and shut her eyes. He knew that every time he took drugs, he would float in air and everything around him would turn hazy. It would bring out all his carnal instincts. Both slept in each other's arms—tired and content.

🔍

Mia Bella
15th September 2013, Around 1 am

'Why did you stop? I want to know what happened after that and I am sure everyone here wants to know too,' I said curiously.

'Aditya, don't be so loud. Your voice will reach downstairs,' Sakshi pinched me.

Some stories steal your heart, some give you goosebumps, while some fill the air with romance. But only some stories have all the elements. I was listening to one such story. There were different things going on in my mind. Who was the girl that Vikrant had seen a couple of times in the metro? What was going on in Anamika's mind when she said yes to Anurag? What was going to happen to Sanaya? When everything seemed fine, what made Vikrant take up the job of singing in Mia Bella? While listening to Vikrant's story, I realized I hadn't moved an inch. I don't think anyone else sitting there had even realized it was raining slightly till Vikrant had stopped.

'Is there something wrong?' Sakshi asked Vikrant.

'Can I freshen up and come back? I need to use the washroom,' he asked.

I nodded. What was strange was that no one had even touched their drinks while Vikrant was narrating the story. It just went on to show how exciting the story was. Loving someone can either take you to dizzying heights or spoil your life forever. I was confused whether Yuvi was going to reach those heights or would he become hazy? To me, his life seemed smooth with a perfect girlfriend like Kashish.

'Would you like to eat something?' Sakshi asked me. I was lost deeply in thoughts. I got up from my chair and went towards the corner of the bar to smoke. Till date, I had heard about complexities in a college band. I had also witnessed complexities in relationships. But Vikrant and his friend's lives had a different level of complexity to them. Anamika was a bombshell whom you could flaunt around in the college campus to make a few boys jealous. Vikrant was in love with a girl whom he had never met but merely seen a couple of times. He didn't know her whereabouts or whether she was committed. Yuvi and Kashish were stable in their relationship but what was even more important for Yuvi was that he wanted to make their band popular. They already were to some extent. I was still not in a position to comment on Sanaya. Anurag was the luckiest of all because he slept around with a different girl every month. But I felt he had become a changed man after meeting Anamika. Of course, my judgement was based on the basis of what Vikrant had narrated.

Vikrant had come back after his little loo break and took off from where he had left.

'Who was that girl in the metro? Do you really love her? I mean loved her?' I asked out of curiosity.

'Loving someone or not is beyond your control. It didn't take me even a second to realize that she was the one. She was the one who would understand my needs. She was the one who would help me be a better person. She was the one who could make me feel like I was perfect even though I was not. Her smile would enlighten my thoughts every morning. But the more I travelled by the metro, the more I seemed to be lost. I couldn't trace her anywhere after those two times. Maybe she had seen me staring at her and changed her route. That's when I understood that the feelings do not hold value and it was the actual execution of one's feelings that mattered. I had to show my love to her. But she never gave me any signs. My determination was not enough. Not for me at least. You have to let the other person know you like and care for that person. But she just didn't,' said a visibly upset looking Vikrant.

'So your paths never crossed after that?' Sakshi asked.

He just smiled and sipped his drink even though he had told us that he wasn't really fond of it. 'Why have you started drinking?' I questioned.

'Takdeer, my destiny,' he said recalling moments from his past. 'But did Anamika share her intentions behind her relationship?' she added.

'Yes. She did. We understood later why she had a phobia of getting ragged. Why was she told stories about it from the very beginning? The stories were not of any unknown people—they were of her very own elder sister who was tortured so much during college days that she eventually ran away. She was still missing and the Delhi Police had declared her dead by showing her parents one dead body that was not in a recognizable condition. Her experiences in the past had fuelled her fear of ragging and to get temporary relief for her phobia, she had accepted Anurag's proposal. Yuvi and I knew that the senior guys had planned something as horrible as stripping for her. After she told us what had happened to her sister, even we were convinced that Anamika was not wrong. She was not a slut. The situation had forced her to make that decision,' Vikrant added.

'But did the relationship last?' I asked.

'She never wanted it to last. She herself knew that it was not going to last forever. But she held on to it till she could. She enjoyed roaming in Anurag's big car. Moreover, her low attendance didn't matter too. After all her boyfriend was the Student's Union president. Sometimes she would feel bad for keeping Anurag in the dark, but she would keep telling herself it was only a matter of a few days. We just hoped it did not turn ugly in the future because I had heard that Anurag didn't like if anyone hurt his ego.'

'I feel bad for Sanaya who got trapped without her fault. She could have handled things better,' I added.

'She did. She surely did. Till then, I was not aware of anything. I had never seen her nor talked to her. All I knew was she was Anurag's ex-girlfriend and was upset with Anurag and Anamika's relationship even though she had told everyone that she had decided to move on,' Vikrant explained looking at the menu card.

'You won't order anything now. First tell us more about the story,' Anuj, the manager of restaurant, added.

'At least you can bring me something to munch on,' Vikrant requested.

Anuj accepted his request and told the chef to whip something up for us. We were chit-chatting normally till Vikrant heard a fuss downstairs. I got up to see what the chaos was all about.

'Don't worry. That's regular routine. Look at the time. It's 1 am. Some group does all the drama after getting drunk and the police takes them away. So chill. Just let me switch off the lights and close the door otherwise they will create a problem for us too,' Anuj said.

'But you want to sit in darkness?' I asked.

'Sssh. I have a few candles here with me. I am not switching off the fan though,' he whispered.

'Dude, how do you expect the candles to light when the fan is on at full speed?' I laughed.

'Leave it to me.'

I checked the watch and I was dumbstruck to see the time. We were so engrossed that we had forgotten about the world outside. The permit time was over and the police had come to dispel the mob comprising mostly of youngsters downstairs. They were also doing a routine check to see if all the lounges and restaurants had closed. We went inside so that no one could guess we were sitting on the rooftop. I understood then the reason why Anuj had asked for the lights to be switched off. We remained quiet for some time until the noise died down. Anuj once again went towards the corner to make sure the police had left. He came back and gave us two thumbs up to signal everything was fine.

Love can neither be defined nor expressed. The night was such that nobody cared about whether the lights and fans were on or off or whether there was a moon in the sky. You just wanted the night to continue. I was eager to hear the rest of the story. Everyone settled down and Vikrant continued with the story.

'VAYU. Everyone had high hopes from our band. We were becoming popular not only through our shows but also because of our live videos that we had uploaded on our YouTube channel which had gone viral within a couple of weeks. Anamika's popularity on the social media increased with a rapid pace and at the same time music lovers had gone crazy about Yuvi's voice with more than half a million hits on YouTube. We had a show scheduled the coming week and we were preparing day and night for it. Though Yuvi was still a big drug user, we were confident that we would outperform the other groups and give our best performance.'

Just then Vikrant's phone rang. I could make out a girl's voice on the other side. He talked to her for a few seconds and quickly hung up the phone.

'Sorry, she was…leave it. It's not important. So where was I? Our performance and rehearsals….'

The Girl in the Metro

'Vikrant, the beats are off. Let's do it again,' Yuvi suggested.

'Yuvi, let's change the tempo of the song. It will get our brain juices bubbling. What say?' Vikrant counter suggested to which Anamika agreed instantly.

The trio was rehearsing for their upcoming intercollege performance. They wanted to sound unique—different from all the other bands out there. The show was hardly a few days away and they wanted to give their performance all that they had.

'So the song goes like, *Naseeba…Naseeba…ye meri life hai…naseeba naseeba…*' sang Anamika.

'Let me try singing it once,' Vikrant said.

'*Naseeeeebaaa, ye meri life hai…*Na, this tune is not right. Let's go back to the first version,' Yuvi added.

They had loaded up on snacks, beers, soda, marijuana, and cigarettes. Though they were kept hidden in a bag, Miss Malini got a whiff of it but she didn't scold them because she wanted the show to go on perfectly well. After trying out various versions of the song, Yuvi suggested to stick to the basics and not to try to be too innovative with their title song 'Naseeba'.

'Let's sing Dhaani once again. Yuvi, you start first. I will join in the chorus. Let's practice as if a live show is going on,' Vikrant said.

'Dhaani…re Dhaaniiiii..chunariya… Dhaani…re dhaani… chunariya… Udte baadal ke saaye me lehraayegi, mujhe tadpaayegi, chali jaayegi, jaise bijuriaa…mastaanii…'

Once satisfied with their demo performance, all of them hugged each other and sat on the stage wiping off the sweat from their brows.

'The song was worth recording, dude. If we keep putting in the same amount of effort into each performance, we will surely make waves with our music. It's so much fun,' said Yuvi relaxing on the floor. He shut his eyes dreaming of their live performance where a big crowd had gathered and people were shouting his name over and over again, screaming their heart out.

Vikrant opened beer bottles for them while Yuvi rolled a paper. This time they wanted to rehearse like real rock stars. Vikrant drank a Bacardi breezer. Yuvi teased him saying only sissy girls drank breezers. Vikrant didn't take Yuvi's words to heart because he knew Yuvi was merely joking.

'Give me a drag. Let me show you how it's actually done. I am not a first timer. I have tried everything once but I don't get addicted to stuff like you,' Vikrant bluffed.

'Oh, is it so? Then show it to me, baby. This is not a candy, darling,' Yuvi laughed and Anamika joined in.

'I find a girl who smokes really sexy. Such girls are not afraid of midnight parties. They are not afraid of hitting the dance floor and rapping with you. These chicks don't always sit in class and talk shit,' Yuvi said provoking Anamika.

Vikrant snatched the roll from Yuvi's hand and took a drag. Then another, another…till he could barely get up from his seat. He could not even speak. He probably could not understand what was happening around him. Yuvi had told him 'Beta, slowly…one at a time.' But Vikrant wanted to prove he was man enough to do it. They were enjoying this new phase of life. All three of them had become really good friends with each other and their bonding was inseparable. Still Yuvi held some grudges against Anamika but she always won his faith back. They kept rehearsing day in and day out with on the same energy and enthusiasm. Yuvi was now more confident about the show because all the band members were performing at their optimal best. They all laughed, did masti, and practiced! Soon, they were all set for the D-day.

18th August, 2012

'Ladies and gentleman, it gives me immense pleasure to host this show today. To my utter delight, I got to meet a particular band backstage. Any guesses whom I am talking about?' said the host building up the excitement.

VAYU…VAYU…VAYU!!!

'There you are. Absolutely right. I am talking about VAYU. The band that has reached the peak of popularity in only a couple of months' time. I can see many of you wearing T-shirts with VAYU written on it. So let me present to you the students who make up your very favourite band—VAYUUUUUUU. First up is the lead guitarist and vocalist Yuvi. The Y of VAYU.'

Yuvi was busy kissing Kashish and did not hear his name being announced. Ultimately Kashish pushed him on stage. Yuvi waved at the audience as the lights fell on him to mark his entry. As he took to the centre of the stage, the host continued, 'Now it's time to call out the V of VAYU. Let me hear you scream for the lead drummer and lyricist Vikrant.'

Vikrant touched the stage with his right hand and then touched his forehead. By doing this, he was asking for the blessings of the almighty before performing on a platform he had dreamt of all his life. He took his position and played the drums a little to get the audience in the groove.

'And now let me call upon the last member of the group—the beautiful lady of VAYU. The girl who has become every guy's dream. She is the A of VAYU. Let's give a shout out to Anamika, the dancer of the band.'

As Anamika came on stage, the crowd went crazy shouting her name. She looked ravishing in pink shorts and a black top. The lights made her look even sexier. The audience whistled loudly and called out her name. Yuvi seemed upset because of the attention Anamika was getting. Being the lead vocalist, he wanted to be the centre of attention but that wasn't happening. He put his grudges behind him and addressed the audience after the host had left the stage.

'Are you ready to have the time of your life?' Yuvi screamed. The crowd responded with double the enthusiasm. 'Okay then, this one is for all the people in love. This is our version of a song you all love. Put your hands in the air. Here it goes. To all the aashiqs and their aashiqui...' Yuvi announced.

Yuvi closed his eyes for a split second and started crooning...

Kal raat ek beshakal ki...awaaz ne mujhe chauka diya,
Maine kaha tu kaun hai...usne kaha,
Aawaargi!!
Ye dil ye paagal dil mera...kyu bhuj gaya,
Aawaargi!!

Ek ajnabee jhoke ne jab...pucha mere gam ka sabab,
sehra ki bheegi ret par...maine likha
Aawaargi!!
Is dasht mein ek shehar tha...woh kya hua?
Aawargi!!

The performance created complete havoc! The crowd screamed like crazy. It was the best performance of their lives. They performed on various songs like Aawargi. Vikrant played the drums to perfection while Yuvi's voice left everybody mesmerized. To add to it, Anamika's moves set the stage on fire. It was one hell of a show for the audience and they were going to remember it for ages. All the boys in the crowd were imaging themselves with Anamika while all the girls were fantasizing about either Yuvi or Vikrant. After the performance got over, they bowed in front of everyone and left the stage. The crowd kept chanting ONCE MORE, ONCE MORE, but since other colleges had to perform as well, their wish wasn't granted. One by one the other college bands performed, but their performances were lacklustre as compared to VAYU. It was VAYU all the way. The trio partied all night to celebrate their success. But every time Anamika talked about how good she danced that night, Yuvi's temper would flare up. He was the lead performer of the band and wanted to get the maximum attention. He had expected the audience to applaud for him the most. He had somewhere started to hate her. He knew Anamika was a pretty looking girl and in a way deserved the popularity she got. This was the only reason he kept mum about it. He also didn't want to spoil the party.

They were not just popular, they were loved by all the students of Delhi University. They got countless Facebook friend requests and their YouTube videos had gone completely viral. The entire University was talking about VAYU and the three were visible everywhere. Their songs were being played in buses, autos, and the metro.

With more shows under their belt, their popularity kept growing. But on the downside, Yuvi's differences with Anamika increased as well. Anamika had no clue why Yuvi would behave strangely around her. She felt like he was unhappy with her about something but didn't dare ask him what. Her popularity was killing Yuvi from inside. Vikrant calmed him down whenever he was about to lose control. But his grievances against Anamika didn't affect Yuvi's performances. Instead, it got better with every passing show.

As the days passed, they managed to get many sponsors for their stage shows. They were living their dream. Their immense hard work had eventually paid off. Even their college was extremely proud of them and let them sit for exams despite having low attendance. Even the sponsors made good profits from the shows. With every show, their popularity kept increasing. They had become one of the most known music groups in Delhi.

Auditorium, Rajhans College
22nd August, 2012

VAYU was preparing for their next show which was going to happen in their college itself for an event organized by the seniors. The seniors had requested them to sing some special songs for their performance. The enthusiasm was at its peak. The band members were backstage getting ready for the show. Vikrant wanted to beat his previous acts and had requested Yuvi to give him a drug to consume as he felt he gave his best performance when he was high. He recalled an earlier time he had consumed drugs after which he had given his best performance. Yuvi took it very casually and gave him a small packet containing marijuana from his pocket. Vikrant took out a small paper from his pocket and emptied the contents on the paper. He then rolled it up.

'This helps you, right?' Vikrant asked before lighting the roll.

'Yes. You very well knew that I smoke before every show. Don't you? Come on now, don't be a kid. Take a puff,' Yuvi added.

Vikrant was feeling awkward doing it around Yuvi, so he went to the dressing room instead. By the time he came out, he was feeling very high.

'Are you alright?' Anamika asked Vikrant. She was concerned about his health and could sense something fishy going on.

'Baby boy is on drugs,' Yuvi teased him.

Yuvi was so used to taking drugs on a regular basis that it was a routine matter for him. He thus could understand it was the first time for Vikrant and he was having a hard time dealing with it.

'I am alright,' Vikrant said trying hard not to close his eyes.

He peeped into the auditorium to see how many people had gathered so far. It was a packed house. His eyes were getting heavier with each passing second as a result of the drug and as he tried to take the support of a pillar nearby, his eyes fell on the girl. The same girl he had spotted in the metro! She was standing right next to the stage and applauding the band. Dressed in a red one-piece dress, she looked extremely sexy. She was screaming, smiling, and enjoying herself at the same time. Suddenly, their eyes met. Just when he raised his hand to wave at her, she turned the other way. He tried to regain composure as his performance was due to start in a few minutes. He was already feeling unhinged from the marijuana. Just then an idea struck him! He thought of proposing to her right there. Though it needed guts, he had never been more sure of anything before this. And he anyway had nothing to lose. He didn't even know if he could see her again or not. He wondered if they were from the same college. If yes, then why hadn't he seen her in college ever? No, she must be an outsider. How could she get entry into the college? The show was just for seniors. Was she his senior? Before he could get his answers, he saw his girl walking away from the stage talking to someone on the phone. Vikrant became restless. He couldn't take the fact that the girl was walking away. The drug was showing its effect. The more stress he took, the more unhinged he felt. Those few seconds felt like an hour for him. Without even giving it a second thought, he got down from the stage. Yuvi and Anamika were surprised to see him leave even before their performance had begun. They were clueless and didn't know how to react. They had no option but to continue with the show without Vikrant, even if it meant facing the seniors' anger. Vikrant left abruptly without informing anyone.

Without caring about anything, he ran after the metro girl who had left the college premises in a hurry. He saw her get into an auto. He hurriedly waved out to another approaching auto.

After getting in, he told the auto driver, 'Bhaiya, us auto ke peeche chalo.'

The auto stopped outside Vishwavidyala metro station. Seeing her get out, Vikrant got out too. He was careful to stand at a few meters distance from her lest she sees him following her. His phone kept ringing but he didn't care to pick it up. He thanked his stars that his phone was on silent mode else his cover would have been blown off. Anamika and Yuvi were both calling him continuously. They sent him numerous text messages. But he ignored all of them. Both of them got into the same metro without the girl knowing about it. She had no clue someone was following her. He kept some distance from her and watched her like a love-struck boy. She was busy listening to songs on her iPod. He saw a few guys purposely trying to touch her or brush their body against hers, which annoyed her a great deal. More than her, Vikrant was annoyed but he didn't let his anger show because he did not want to create a scene in the metro. She got down at Saket and he continued with his chase. Then he saw her get into an apartment. That was it. She disappeared in a second and he was left staring at the empty road.

What do I have to do to get noticed by you? Change my hair, change my clothes, change the way I walk, or change the way I talk? It's been a while since we have known to each other—at least I know you—yet I am invisible to you. Your one look makes me go weak in the knees. It takes me to a place that I can't even describe. Is it wrong if I want more of you? I knew the day I saw you that we were meant to be together. It's our destiny…then why is it taking so much time for us to come together? What should I do to make you realize how much I love you? How desperately I wish you come to your apartment's terrace right now and give me a flying kiss. I left my show for you but still you are not aware of my feelings. Why? What do I have to do to get noticed by you?

A tear came rolling down his cheek as he looked at his reflection in the mobile screen. Why wasn't he able to gather the courage to talk to her? What was holding him back? He left his show abruptly and ran from there to approach her, to talk with her, to share his feelings with her but he did nothing. As he walked back towards the college, he realized what a blunder he had made. He immediately took out his mobile phone and checked his messages. There were many. He opened one of them sent by Yuvi.

Dude, what happened to you? I didn't expect this from you. Do you realize how important this show was for us? Anyway, we have left the college premises. The show has been cancelled.

The last line kept reverberating in his mind. *The show has been cancelled.* He didn't know how to react. He felt guilty and called Yuvi to apologize to him but Yuvi's cell was unavailable. He decided to tell Yuvi and Anamika the truth. He walked back alone helplessly. All he could do was to wish that things would fall in place once again.

An Ending and a Beginning

'What do you think of yourself? Were you out of your mind? Do you even know what you have done and how badly it has affected our band's image? I am getting so many messages about our cancelled show. Everybody is asking us for a valid reason to justify your abrupt escape. What am I supposed to tell everyone?' screamed Yuvi at the top of his voice. 'Will you fucking care to speak up?'

Anamika was standing beside Vikrant while Yuvi gave him an earful. Vikrant, Yuvi, and Anamika had met later in the night after the cancellation of the show on Vikrant's request. Vikrant had managed to convince them to meet him by apologizing for his mistake and promising not to repeat it again. He had also convinced them that whatever he did had a strong reason behind it. Anamika consoled him and told him not to worry about it.

'At least tell us what had happened? What was going on in your mind?' she asked holding his hands as a sign of support.

After a long silence, Vikrant spoke teary-eyed, 'I love her. I am crazy about her. I want her anyhow. Help me.'

'Who?' both Anamika and Yuvi asked in chorus.

'That girl.'

'Which girl?' Anamika asked first.

'The metro girl.'

Yuvi and Anamika were getting irritated now. They could not understand what Vikrant was trying to say. This continued for some more time until Vikrant told them about the girl he had seen in the metro a couple of times. They were surprised to hear that Vikrant had a crush on a girl. According to him, it was love.

'Dude, are you still on drugs? I mean, you have not even talked to her, you don't even know her name, and she hardly knows about you—except from the fact that you're part of a band. That's all she knows. You also don't know much about her expect for where she lives. Grow up. I don't want you to get into all these complications.'

'What's my fault, Yuvi? Aren't you in a relationship? Did I ever tell you to stop fucking around? No, right? Then how can you say this to me? I am saying that I really like that girl. Yes, I am confused about a few things but I want to give it a try. Just when I need you people the most, you are demotivating me,' said Vikrant losing his temper.

'We are with you Vikrant. Now forget everything and let's chill out for the day and then plan the best way to approach your girl,' Anamika said patting his back.

We never choose love, love chooses us. It is that unpredictability that makes the journey so worth it. In every age, in every place, love is certain to be there; Vikrant had found it in that girl. He felt like he had searched his whole life and had finally found the one meant for him. Life on earth is just that brief moment you spend with your loved one. Meeting that stranger had made him realize how precious and fragile life can be. He could give up everything for that one moment with her, for that one moment would be better than a lifetime of never knowing her. He could not imagine a life without her now and wanted to meet her again. He was happy that his friends had understood him and were willing to help him out of this situation. Yuvi though was upset with whatever had happened but he let it pass because even he loved someone. However, he warned not only Vikrant but even Anamika to be very professional and not let such things hamper their success. Many dream to achieve what they had and Yuvi didn't want to lose it due to a small mistake. They all hugged each other as a sign of support and togetherness. Anamika kept forcing Yuvi and Vikrant to come along for a day's trip with her and Anurag.

'No yaar, you both go. I will join you guys some other time,' Vikrant said.

'Yuvi, at least you come with us. You can bring Kashish along if you want. It will be fun. Then even I can spend some time with you and get to know you more.'

'You want your boyfriend to kill me?' Yuvi added.

'Won't Kashish kill me?' Anamika asked and they all laughed.

'Come on, Yuvi. Now, don't make excuses. At least you should come,' said Anamika tried to convince him.

'What will we do there? Neither Kashish nor I know Anurag much. I mean we are not friends with him,' Yuvi asked puzzled.

'Shut up. You know me, that is enough. You come along for me and not for him. And obviously I will introduce you both to him. You will not feel like strangers. Trust me,' she said excitedly.

After lot of convincing, Yuvi finally agreed to go along with Kashish. Vikrant was not in a mood to go. Anamika was excited that at least Yuvi was joining them. But before agreeing, he had put a condition in front of her that if he didn't like Anurag, he would stay away from him. Anamika agreed.

Satyam Cineplex, Nehru Place, Delhi
24th August, 2012

All of them decided to go for a movie to Satyam Cineplex. Yuvi and Anurag were supposed to reach early to buy the tickets. It was an awkward moment when both of them reached almost at the same time and stood one after the other in the ticket counter line. Being from the same college, they vaguely knew of each other but had never got a chance to talk. To avoid embarrassment, Anurag broke the silence.

'Hi. So what's up? We never interacted with each other much. But I hope everything is going well,' Anurag asked Yuvi.

'Indeed. Everything is good. Even the grades are good,' Yuvi replied.

'I hope we both didn't disturb you. I mean you know how Anamika is. She must have forced you to come along, right?'

'Not really.'

'Where is Vikrant? He didn't come?'

'He is in Lapataganj,' Yuvi smiled and said, 'How's it going with Anamika?'

'I am confused as to what it is that she wants from me. You won't believe it but we still haven't taken our relationship to the next level,' he said.

'That's not a big deal,' Yuvi said casually. He believed if you are serious in a relationship and have made up your mind to be with the other person, then the physical act of love does not really matter.

'Yes, I agree. But if you want your relation to sustain for long, you need to get close. Else how would you...you know...' Anurag gestured shrugging his shoulders. Yuvi felt weird talking to Anurag about such intimate matters. He wanted to run away but kept put just for Anamika's sake. He felt that Anurag wanted to take advantage of Anamika and was in the relationship only for sex. On the other hand, he knew that even Anamika was not serious about Anurag. Then why did the relationship last so long? Probably, that's what relationships have become these days. Chalti ka naam gaadi.

Where Yuvi and Anurag were a complete mismatch, Anamika and Kashish gelled along well, especially when the topic of discussion was Yuvi. Though Anamika and Kashish had not interacted with each other ever before, they got along like a house on fire. Kashish was a bit shy when it came to expressing her views. But when the conversation drifted to a discussion on Yuvi, she completely let loose.

'How do you manage to handle his mood swings? He goes crazy once he's doped,' Anamika winked.

'You have not seen the worst of him after doping. I know him better that way and I know how far things can go,' Kashish smiled teasingly.

'Is it? Then I should try it once,' Anamika added.

'No no. He is best suited for me. No one else can handle him the way I do. He is mine,' Kashish said holding Yuvi's hand.

'Who is what? What's going on?' Yuvi asked but Kashish pushed him inside the theatre.

They took their seats. Yuvi and Kashish took the corner seats while Anamika and Anurag came and sat next to them. The lights were put off and the opening credits started rolling on the screen.

As time passed, Yuvi tried to get close to Kashish. Kashish hesitated as Anurag and Anamika were sitting right next to them. But eventually Yuvi managed to seduce Kashish and kissed her passionately on her lips. Anamika was more interested in what was happening in the seats next to her than the actual movie. She saw Yuvi insert his hand into Kashish's top. Anurag had no clue what was happening. He felt Anamika was staring at him in the absence of lights. He put his hands on her shoulder and brought her close. They gazed at each other for a while until Anamika took his arm from her shoulder and placed it back on his lap.

'Now what? Why are you pushing me away?' Anurag asked in frustration.

'Nothing. Please, not here,' Anamika replied.

'Is it the first time we are doing this?' Anurag questioned again.

'Please, not now. Can we just watch the movie, please, like the rest of the audience?' Anamika requested.

'Of course. Anyway, I don't mean anything to you, right? I am a loser. Thanks for letting me know.'

'When did I say that?' Anamika said raising her voice.

To avoid fighting, Anurag kept quiet and did not react further. It would have been embarrassing to fight in front of Yuvi and Kashish, especially when they were having a good time together. Anurag didn't talk to Anamika for the entire movie. On the other side, Yuvi and Kashish's romance was picking up heat to which not only left Anurag but even Anamika feeling insecure. But lovers are lovers! They just look for an opportunity. The movie got over and Yuvi decided to drop Anamika and Anurag home.

'Just stop the car at a nearby restaurant. I want to take a parcel,' Anurag requested Yuvi on the way.

'Sure. Buy some booze as well. You can make the most of it,' Yuvi teased Anamika from the rear-view mirror.

'Thank you for your suggestion,' Anamika said dismissively. She kept looking at him through the same rear mirror while driving the car. Yuvi dropped Kashish at her house and gave her a goodbye kiss at the gate. This made both Anamika and Anurag jealous as they had had a bad fight during the movie. Dropping off Kashish, Yuvi took to the wheel again and finally halted at a good roadside restaurant. Anurag got down to take the parcel while Yuvi and Anamika sat in the car. Yuvi turned back to look at Anamika and gave her a smile.

'What's wrong?' he asked.

'You really love Kashish a lot, right?' she questioned.

'Of course. No other girl has brought me the same amount of joy that she has in my life. I know now that if there was ever someone who could love me and take care of me, it is Kashish. You know what, Anamika? I fall deeper and deeper in love with her every day. The passion in our relationship is still alive,' Yuvi said with a big smile on his face.

Anamika smiled back and looked outside the window.

'What about you?' Yuvi asked.

'Me…me too!' Anamika whispered.

'Really? I thought you were just…with Anurag. Remember you had told me?' Yuvi asked curiously.

'Oh, you are talking about Anurag. I was just kidding. Obviously, I am not serious. We are more like friends than lovers. Did you see me getting intimate with him in the movie hall like Kashish?' Anamika winked.

'Maybe you are too shy or maybe he is not bold,' Yuvi laughed and they gave a high-five to each other.

As their hands touched each other, Yuvi held her hand and said, 'I am sorry.'

'Why are you saying sorry?' she asked.

Yuvi held her hand firmly, rubbing his thumb on the back of her hand. Before they could talk, they saw Anurag walking towards the car. Yuvi immediately let go of her hand. Then on second thoughts, he took her hand again and kissed it to apologize for the wrong things he had thought about her.

'Anurag is watching. He will kill me if he sees you kissing my hand,' Anamika whispered nervously.

'Don't worry, my windows are fully tinted. He can't see what's happening inside,' Yuvi smiled.

'Why did you say sorry?' she asked again.

'Will tell you some other time,' Yuvi replied unlocking the doors of the car.

Anurag got into the car and gave Yuvi directions to his house. An hour later, Yuvi dropped both of them at Anurag's apartment. Yuvi wanted to tell her that somewhere he assumed that she would just go wrong way and spoil the band image. He felt that her not-so-serious relationship would hamper their growth. He also thought that Anamika was that kind of a girl who could sleep around with others for her own benefit. But he was wrong.

He still had doubts about Anurag though. He also wanted to tell her that somewhere he felt attracted towards her. If it was not for Kashish, he would have surely thought of making a move on her. But that wasn't a possibility. Yuvi was trying to build the bonding stronger than before. However, Anurag bumped in between and Yuvi didn't utter a word.

Anurag's Residence, RK Puram, Delhi

'I have brought your favourite brand and your favourite flavour—just to make you feel special,' Anurag stated revealing the contents of the bag he had picked up from the restaurant on their way to his house.

'What the fuck!' Anamika shouted.

'What? You dirty mind. I am talking about Vodka,' he smiled.

He had purchased a vanilla-flavoured Smirnoff Vodka for the night. Anamika loved that flavour and her eyes glittered with happiness. She hugged Anurag for making the evening so special.

'I have something else for you,' Anurag added.

He brought out a greeting card from the bag and gave it to her. Anamika just gazed at him for few seconds before kissing him on his cheek for giving her such a lovely surprise. It had their photo on the front and a picture of Anamika dancing at the back. On the inside, their names were written in a beautiful font on the left and a message on the right. She started reading the text.

I don't know how you will react to this little note of love. You may feel surprised, flattered, or be indifferent. But rest assured, this is my first love letter to any girl. I am not good at words but I will still try to convey my feelings to you. I have been in a relationship in the past but have never felt this way about someone. I am so struck by your innocent, child-like face. This is a small poem for you. Though it hasn't been written by me, it reflects my love towards you.

To my love,

When nothing makes sense and every thought is blurred,
Love will find its way!!
When you look into my eyes, you view my soul.
It is everything I am and because of it,
I will always love you!!
If there was a word to describe my love,
Surely it would only be spoken by God!!
All I have to offer you is me and my love,
Though both are simple, I promise they are true.
Life is truly a mystery,
A puzzle waiting to be solved!
Although one might be able to solve it alone,
The answer will be found easier with another!!
I want to discover life with you Anamika,

And experience all of life's mysteries together in your embrace!!
I love you, dil se!

She closed the greeting card and kept it on the table beside her. The next moment she jumped into Anurag's arms. They hugged tightly for the next few minutes after which Anurag took her to the bedroom for some drinks. He made a Vodka peg with sprite and offered it to Anamika.

'Cheers. This is for our love,' he said raising a toast.

Anamika started feeling awkward as she didn't really love him. Her guilt had caught up with her. She remained quiet and took a sip of the vodka. She had started this relationship just to escape ragging and get over her phobia. But the same relationship was now getting on her nerves as Anurag was trying to come too close to her. She had never imagined Anurag would get serious about her. She gulped her drink down in one go and refilled her glass again.

'Are you fine? Don't drink too much,' Anurag requested.

'Chill. I am fine. Make another one for me,' she ordered putting down the glass after her second shot.

Anurag made another peg which she gulped down again at the speed of lightning. She remained quiet for some time and then turned towards Anurag. She was not in her senses anymore and the alcohol was having its effect on her.

'Do you really love me so much? I mean, I don't. Then how can you?' she said in a low tone.

Anurag took it as a joke and ignored her. But she kept asking the same question again and again. Anurag kept the glasses of vodka aside and came close to her leaving no space. Their thighs rubbed against each other.

'I can't express how much I love you. I agree that I just wanted to show you off in the beginning, but as I got to know the real person behind this hot and sexy figure, I started falling madly and deeply in love with you and now I can't live without you baby. I can fight with everyone to keep you in my life.'

As he said this, Anamika started feeling guiltier. She wanted to tell him everything but she knew how aggressive Anurag could be if he got upset. She kept mum for her own safety. They hugged each other and continued drinking.

'I love you Anamika. You are so sexy and so ravishing. I so want you right now,' Anurag whispered in her ear holding her by her waist.

'I love you too,' Anamika replied.

'Would you mind playing golf tonight?' Anurag teased her.

'Shut up,' Anamika said pinching his shoulders lightly.

Anurag still continued to woo her by caressing her back and kissing her neck. Anamika knew that her neck was her weakest point and whenever anyone touched her neck or licked it, she would lose control easily. Romance in any relationship demands time; it demands being open to feeling loved and wanting to love. But Anamika was not craving love. The more Anurag touched her, the more she turned cautious. She never wanted to get intimate with him and had preserved her womanhood for her prince.

Anurag was surely not the one. Her top fell on the floor and he pulled her skirt up to her thighs but Anamika pulled it down again, opposing Anurag's action. His hands had almost gone inside her skirt reaching for her secret place where he felt warmth and sweat. Anamika stood up in shock and turned to leave. This sudden change in her behaviour pissed Anurag off as he was at the peak of excitement and was longing for more.

'What the fuck is wrong with you? We are couples,' he screamed.

'That doesn't give you the right to do this to me. I don't like all this. You might be used to it but I am not. I am not so drunk that I will allow you to take advantage of the situation,' she screamed louder than him.

'You bloody whore. What do you mean by this? Was I taking advantage? You are my girlfriend God dammit. I did not force you to come here. I brought you here so that we could share this moment and take our relationship further.' Anurag couldn't control his anger anymore and hurled the air conditioner remote at Anamika. Luckily, she escaped unhurt.

'That's it. I am going. I can't stay here anymore,' she stated.

Anurag got up and went closer to her. He held her so tightly by her arms that it almost hurt her. Tears came rolling down her eyes. But Anurag ignored it and kept shouting at her. Every passing second his grip on her arms got stronger, hurting her even more.

'Please, I want to go. I am not feeling well. What do you want me to do? Sleep with you on this bed? That I should obey your orders and lose my virginity?' she asked.

'Oh please. Don't tell me you are a virgin. Girl like you can't be a virgin,' he shouted again.

Anamika pushed him aside. This time, his words had really hurt her. For a split second, she felt as if she was really a slut. For a split second, she feared losing her virginity. But she managed to escape his grip and immediately left the place. She didn't even wipe her tears or comb her hair. Her eyeliner had spread all over her face leaving black marks near her eyes. Anurag tried hard to stop her but all in vain.

Her self-esteem was shattered. She was left void and empty. She knew this was coming but she didn't expect it to come this way. Anurag tried hard to express to her that he didn't want her only to satisfy his physical needs and that he really loved and cared for her. When a relationship fails, it hurts. But when you fail a person, it hurts even more. On her way back, she kept comparing how Yuvi treated his girlfriend with so much care and how brutally Anurag treated her.

Why do we blame ourselves when the other person decides to cheat on us or force himself on us? Why does it make us think that we are not worthy of love? Both of them thought that night that they were not worthy of love.

Happiness is a Whore

Lover's Point, aka Canteen, Rajhans College
27th August, 2012

It's never easy for a heart to find an easy path. It wanders every time. In all relationships, someone's sentiments get hurt. Certain expectations remain unfulfilled. When these expectations are ignored or left unfulfilled, a sense of betrayal overcomes us. However, the truth is that if we put our heart aside for a moment, we realize that our partner was not even aware of these expectations that needed fulfilment in the first place.

Anurag had some expectations from Anamika and wanted to see them fulfilled. But when his expectations were shattered, it hurt his ego. It was probably the first time a girl had categorically rejected his advances Earlier, it was always him who broke up with the girl and never the other way around. Anamika had wanted it to be a light-hearted passing affair. She hadn't expected things to get so serious. Her expectations were hurt too. These expectations are probably driven by notions in a person's mind about how a perfect lover behaves. There is no harm in having such expectations of your partner. However, if we expect our partner to fulfil them every time, then it's our duty to let them know what we expect from the relationship and not assume they will know it by themselves.

Anamika should have talked to him about his expectations quite early to avoid all the chaos. Now she was hurt. It was visible from her face. Vikrant sensed it when they both were eating snacks in the canteen.

'Is anything the matter? Why are your eyes so swollen?' Vikrant asked her with a concerned expression.

'Nothing.'

'Did Anurag say anything to you? Or Yuvi?'

She couldn't hold it in anymore and started weeping in the canteen in front of everyone. Vikrant took her near a corner and asked her what had happened exactly. She narrated everything that had happened the day before in the movie hall as well as at Anurag's place. Vikrant tried his best to comfort her and gave her a shoulder to cry on. He kept making her remember the real reason behind her relationship and advised her to forget about it and move on.

'Just because he said wrong stuff about you doesn't mean it's true. You don't need to prove yourself to anyone. If you hardly care about that person, then why are you fussing over it so much? People will keep making wrong allegations at you. You just have to listen from one ear and take it out from the other. If they have a dirty mind, then so be it. We can't start thinking like them. Then what will be the difference between them and us? Just chill. You deserve someone better,' Vikrant consoled her.

'I never slept with…' muttered Anamika but Vikrant cut her short.

'I know you very well. Even Yuvi doesn't know you as well as me. So relax Anamika. I just said that you don't need to prove yourself to anyone. Those who are your true friends will always believe in you. Just show the middle finger to all the rest. They don't deserve to be in your life.'

'I am hurt not because Anurag didn't try to stop me or ask if I reached home, I am hurt because he thought I was a slut. I have never done such a thing in my life! He was hurling wrongful accusations at me. If you would have been in my place, you would have known how difficult it was for me to overcome the fear of ragging. How difficult it was to tell my parents not to worry about me and that they won't lose their other child too,' she said sobbing loudly.

'This is just a temporary phase. Don't think too much about it. See, even I am single. You can go out with me if you want. We both go to the same college and we both love music. We have amazing chemistry,' Vikrant teased her trying to lighten the mood.

'Vikrant shut up. What will happen to your metro girl then? She will run away even before you make the first move,' Anamika said managing to smile a little.

'So what? I will try my first kiss on you. You can teach me the correct way to do it. Come on, let's try. Your place or mine?' Vikrant said holding her hand firmly.

'Stop it, you asshole.' She pinched him hard on his arms.

'I love you Anamika. I really do. I am your prince charming,' Vikrant kept teasing her all the way to the gate of the college. 'Anamika… No one will love you more than me. Trust me.'

She threw small pebbles at him in protest. Vikrant smiled and hugged her. He had managed to make her smile. Anamika shed the last tear and left the college premises with Vikrant. They headed towards the metro station. Vikrant pulled her cheeks and her ponytail.

You live and learn from every mistake you make. Anamika had learnt a few things like overcoming her fear. Though she was expecting Anurag to call her and pounce on her, that didn't happen. Vikrant stood by her and supported her by telling her that she was different in her own unique way and that her tattoos were extremely seductive. Anamika didn't take his compliments seriously as she knew Vikrant said all those crazy things just to make her smile. She had found a friend of a lifetime in Vikrant. No other friend could do what he did for her—no matter how weird it seemed. They always had fun together and no other friend could understand her better. True friendship like theirs should be treasured forever. And they not only did that but also respected each other's feelings and lifestyle.

'I never thought travelling in the metro would be so blissful. And never in my wildest fantasy did I imagine that I would meet my girl in the metro. A girl whose name is also a mystery for me right now,' Vikrant said to Anamika entering the metro.

'It's okay, baby. I am there for you.'

It was Anamika's turn to tease him now. He looked around to see if he could spot that gorgeous face again but she was nowhere to be seen. Then to his luck, he saw the same girl running towards the metro they had boarded. To his relief, she was able to get on the metro just before the doors shut. Luckily, they were in the same compartment. His heart skipped a beat. He couldn't believe his luck. For a second, he thought he was daydreaming.

'She is here. Oh God, she is here. Fuck! Fuck! I wish I could talk to her,' Vikrant whispered into Anamika's ears.

'Who? Are you drunk?' she asked.

'Yaar, the same girl. The metro girl. She is here.'

'Where?'

'The girl standing at the connecting door. The one in blue,' Vikrant muttered in excitement.

She was dressed in a blue salwar kameez. Her smooth skin glowed in the yellow light and her flawless eyes shone. As she tied her hair into a ponytail, he kept gazing at her, mesmerized by her actions.

'Are you sure that's her?' Anamika was confused.

'Of course, I am,' Vikrant blushed.

'Dumbass. Do you even know that she is from our college? She is our senior,' Anamika exclaimed.

Of course she was! All the pieces of the puzzle fit perfectly now. That's why she could enter the college premises during the show and got entry to their performance and that's why he always saw her take the metro.

'How do you know?' he asked.

'It's a long story. This is not the time to discuss it. Let's talk to her. It's now or never,' Anamika said getting up from her seat.

Vikrant's heartbeats increased and he felt like the blood would come oozing out of his veins any moment. As she went near her, he thought of hiding behind the crowd so she couldn't see him because he feared rejection. Anamika caught hold of him by the collar and dragged him along. They were now standing face to face with the metro girl. He got goosebumps as their eyes met for the second time. It was for the first time he was seeing her so close. He wanted to take her in his arms, hug her, kiss her, and tell her *'You are the one I was looking for and now that I have found you don't go away from me. Don't ignore my request and be with me forever! I will always love you passionately—just the way you want. Will you be my better half?'*

'Hi. I am Anamika. From the band VAYU. I hope you've heard of me,' she declared and waited for her response.

'What do you want?' she replied.

Vikrant was stunned. Such a cold reaction from his dream girl? The one who looked so cute and innocent? Looking at her, no one could predict she would be so rude with a stranger who was talking to her for the first time. Or maybe not! A thought struck him. Why did Anamika say that she knew her? Did the two have a connection?

'I want to talk to you. May I? If you permit,' Anamika added.

'Tell me fast. I don't have time,' she replied again in the same rude tone.

Vikrant was hearing his dream girl's voice for the first time but somehow he didn't like the tone.

'Look, I know that you are aware of everything. But you are taking things the wrong way. He is not serious about this relationship,' Anamika stated and looked at Vikrant.

'What the fuck!' Vikrant muttered.

'Sssh. Let me talk,' Anamika interrupted and continued, 'Believe me, he is not serious about this relationship and nor can he get serious with anyone. He just wants… Leave it. I am here to talk about something else,' Anamika said in a husky voice.

Anamika had left Vikrant completely speechless, clueless, and motionless. What was happening was beyond him.

'Please, can you be a little quick? I don't have so much time,' she muttered again.

Her rudeness was getting on Vikrant's nerves and he finally broke the silence. He knew that if he did not speak at that moment, she would think he was a coward and would never take him seriously.

'Actually, I wanted to have a word with you. Can we be friends? Or slightly more than that? Don't take this the wrong way,' Vikrant stammered.

She understood what Anamika and Vikrant were trying to say. It really pissed her off and she remained silent for a minute. This silence was probably an indication of something horrible coming Vikrant's way. After a lot of hesitation, she finally spoke. Rather pounced on her.

'Look Anamika. Whatever you have done is enough. Now I don't want your sympathy. Please leave me alone. There is no need to introduce me to strangers showing you care. I am not so desperate that I will go around sleeping with the first boy I meet. As you know, I have already faced a lot because of you. Now I don't want any more trouble. So please stay out of my way,' she shouted.

'You are misunderstanding me. Please...' Anamika replied but was interrupted in between.

'I told you to stay away. Do you get that or not? It's because of you that I got insulted so badly. Because of you that bastard slapped me. If you would not have come in between us, Anamika, I would have still been Anurag's girlfriend. It was all because of you, you bitch. Don't try to play these mind games with me. Did Anurag send you saying Sanaya is hurt and please look for some decent guy for him? You thought that you would introduce me to this guy who is popular because of your band and I would readily say yes? Oh please! I am not as cheap as you. So STAY AWAY!'

As she tried to run away, Anamika held her hand and pulled her back. The other people in the metro were having a good time at their expense. After a long list of accusations and blame games, they parted ways. Moments later, their station arrived and both Anamika and Vikrant got down. Her name hit him hard. Sanaya. He had heard it from Yuvi. He didn't expect Sanaya to be the girl in the metro! All his dreams were shattered in a second.

Sanaya! Sanaya! Sanaya! Anurag's Ex-Girlfriend. He kept repeating those words over and over again. The picture was now clear. How badly he wished to be there in the canteen when Yuvi had met Anurag's Ex-girlfriend Sanaya. That very moment he would have known his dream girl was none other than Sanaya! Firstly, Anamika had decided to move on from Anurag and now if Vikrant would have approached Sanaya, Anurag would have lost it. How unfair was destiny. There is a saying 'Out of sight, out of mind.' But that did not hold true for Sanaya. His dream girl was out of his sight, but he couldn't get her out of his mind. He had started loving her and erasing all those dreams in a day was impossible for him.

Anamika was caught in between all the mess. She felt that because of her, Vikrant's love story had ended even without beginning. She ended hers with Anurag on her own will. Sanaya unnecessarily cursed her without knowing the reality. If Anurag was violent with Sanaya then he was violent with Anamika too. It's her luck she managed to escape in time! Her relationship with Anurag had become a barrier for Vikrant.

One moment is all it takes for your world to collapse, crash, and then burn. Happiness is a whore. It lures you in and before you know it, you're spreading your legs for her. And it fucks you. Leaves you hurt and devastated.

🔎

Mia Bella
15th September, 2013, Around 3.30 am

'Oh gosh! That metro girl was Sanaya! You had absolutely no clue she was from your college? I mean you had never seen her in the college premises?' I asked him with a look of surprise.

'I know it's strange. But I never paid attention to anyone in college apart from my band group and a few classmates. So knowing about her was next to impossible. We had so many students in our batch itself that I never interacted with and Sanaya was from our senior batch. So there was no possibility of me knowing her,' Vikrant added.

'But Yuvi never told you?' Sakshi questioned.

'We never discussed this topic in detail. Rather, I never told them about it. The only time I discussed her with them was when I had walked out on the performance before the show to follow her and had to justify my sudden departure to them later. They were not even aware that I loved some girl they knew about,' Vikrant replied taking the last sip of his drink.

The three of them were experiencing so many things in such a short space of time that the listeners were bowled over.

Every decision that we take leads us down a different road. Every decision has some significant impact on our life. Vikrant didn't have any choice. He had to make a decision whether to proceed ahead in his love story or apply breaks to it. He had to be sure about his decision as it would have a deep impact on their lives.

We cannot beg someone to stay if they want to leave. Love doesn't give us the license to own a person. When a relationship of love is developed, a bond of trust is formed. There is an unspoken agreement that the two are committed to each other and will not cheat. So when one of them chooses to be intimate with another person, they break all the bonds of trust. Sanaya felt the same as Anurag had cheated on her with Anamika. Within no time he had switched over to someone else, like he was just waiting for their relationship to end. Did he find something in Anamika that was missing in Sanaya? Sanaya had even moved on but thinking of the memories still hurt. She was not yet aware that Anurag had tried to hurt Anamika.

'You did not approach Sanaya after that?' Sakshi asked.

'I thought we would land in a big mess if I approached her. I still loved her and wanted her to be mine even after knowing that she was my senior and Anurag's ex-girlfriend. I was ready to accept her the way she was because I knew that she was hurt and had gone through a lot at that time. I thought about her situation and realized she wasn't to be blamed for it. Anyone else would have reacted the same way.'

'You are one strong champ. To accept the things as they are is never easy. You still craved for Sanaya's love. I respect such people in my life as I know how it feels when your loved ones walk away from your life,' I said getting sentimental.

We are made up of different personas and to show your real self to the world is always difficult. To accept reality is a challenge. But life brings you to a stage where you need to accept the hardest of truths and move on for those who still love you and want you in their lives. Vikrant was one of them. He knew that Sanaya was Anurag's girlfriend and taking a chance on her would be risky for the entire band. He decided to take a back seat but didn't erase her thoughts completely from his mind.

'Did Anamika break up with Anurag that night?' Sakshi asked Vikrant.

'Anamika didn't like the way Anurag treated her. She was not a sex toy, God dammit. He had tried to get physical with her against her will. Now that's not the right way to prove your manhood or treat your girlfriend. He later on claimed that he truly loved Anamika and was sorry for that night but Anamika didn't give a fuck.'

'You mean he approached her later?' I asked curiously.

'Yes. He did. Not the next day. Anamika expected him to approach her the next day but that didn't happen. In fact on Monday, 27th August, we met Sanaya in the metro as I told you before. I knew things would get worse. Anamika had unknowingly disclosed to Sanaya that she never wanted a long-term relationship. Sanaya wanted an opportunity to show her superiority over Anurag and she got that.'

'How bitchy is that. Why the hell did she tell Anurag about it when she hardly cared?' I shouted.

'Girls will be girls, after all,' he smiled and continued, 'Ask Sakshi what she would have done in case she would have got to know that her ex-boyfriend was dating a girl who never loved him but just used him as a protective shield? She would have told him he was a loser. Sanaya did the same.'

I still wondered what Sanaya was going to gain from it. I guessed that this would be the only reason that the band performance got screwed. I was curious to know Anurag's reaction.

'Then what happened? Did Anurag hit...' I asked but Vikrant interrupted.

'No. He tried to. As he got to know the dark reality behind their relationship, he approached Anamika the next day with his group of friends. He abused her badly and tried to pounce on her. Yuvi was unavailable that time in college but luckily I was present. There were some blows exchanged and before the situation could get worse, some students stopped both parties. Anurag left the place and didn't come in her way again. Anamika didn't react to the entire scenario but was worried about how Yuvi would react once he came to know about it.'

'Oh yes. He had already warned her many times,' Sakshi said.

'I think Yuvi and Kashish were the luckiest. They had a smooth relationship and everything was going well. Isn't it?' I smiled.

'Yes. You are right. They were one such couple whom you could look up to. Kashish stood by him whenever he needed her and that is what you expect from your love,' Vikrant added.

Taking care of a man is not a tough job. All you need to do is pamper him and stay by him when he needs you. No other special gifts are needed. However, taking care of a woman is a challenging job. This is especially true if you are her boyfriend and trying to figure out what she wants. Yuvi had managed to do that for a long period. Anamika wished for someone like Yuvi who could lighten her life. Vikrant craved for his love Sanaya to walk into his life and make his life worth living. Sanaya had moved on but was not ready to accept Vikrant's proposal. Anurag was suffering the same pain of betrayal that he had given to other girls in the past. Now when he had really started loving Anamika, he had got a slap on his face. The sound of that slap echoed so loudly that it hurt his ego.

None of us knew whether they would really be together or end upalone. If they did meet, then what would be the outcome?

'Vikrant, tell me one thing. Did all this affect your band? What happened later?'

'Yes it did. It not only affected us, it ripped us apart.' He closed his eyes and I could see tears rolling down.

From 'Love You' to 'Fuck You'

Have you ever wondered why we always think we will look back at our tears and laugh but never think we will look back at our laughter and cry? Vikrant wanted Sanaya to at least give him a chance to express himself. He was not like those guys who would stamp on her heart and walk away. If someone had looked inside his heart, he would have seen the wounds she had left behind. But rejection had only made him stronger and he waited for the right moment to strike a conversation with her.

A person who rips your heart into pieces by playing with your feelings forgets that there could be a person who could tear him apart too. Anurag was heartbroken and wanted to prove his love to Anamika even though his ego was badly hurt. He somehow kept a check on his anger and decided to approach Anamika once.

Yuvi too came to know about Anamika's break up but didn't really raise the topic with her or with anyone else. Was it because of his fear of getting attracted to Anamika? Or because of her increasing popularity which made him a bit jealous? He never showed any disrespect towards her and preferred to keep a safe distance from her as he knew the sacrifices Kashish had made for him.

As the days passed, their college life sailed on smoothly with college tests, fests, and dhamaal masti. VAYU was gaining popularity all over the city. Vikrant, Anamika, and Yuvi had become the favourites of the entire university and their fan pages on social networking sites gained popularity rapidly. Their wall was full of fan posts and Anamika's wall was full of comments like 'I love you', 'How cute', and 'Sexy lady, wanna go out on a date with me?'. Yuvi envied her for this though it helped in the band's popularity.

'Anamika, let me drop you. It's getting dark,' Yuvi offered.

It was around 9 pm and both Anamika and Yuvi had stayed back in the college for some work. Yuvi offered to drop Anamika home as he thought it was not safe for her to go back alone at such a late hour. Anamika agreed and got into the car.

'Thanks,' she said with a smile on her face.

'Don't be so formal. You think I was going to let you travel alone so late, especially in a place like Delhi?' He looked at her when he spoke and opened the door of his car to let her in.

'So are you ready for the music competition? I hope we bring home the trophy this year,' Yuvi said.

'Yes. I know we will do it. We just need to give our best shot. It will be an important day for us.'

In the coming week, they had to give a live performance at a music festival and on the basis of that, the best band would win the trophy. Rajhans College wanted to win the trophy that year anyhow and they were banking on VAYU for it. It was cold outside and Yuvi had switched on the heater in the car. Once it got warm, Anamika removed her coat and kept it on the back seat. Yuvi turned to look at Anamika. She was wearing skin-fit denims and a red tube top. Her red highlights sparkled under the lights. Yuvi looked at her as if he was seeing her for the first time.

'Why are you staring at me?' asked Anamika.

Yuvi just smiled and said, 'What happened between you and Anurag? Even though you didn't mention anything to me, Vikrant told me everything.'

'Yes, I just told him that it didn't last long. Anyway, chuck it. It was anyhow not supposed to last that long,' Anamika replied casually.

'You really think so? Actually it lasted longer than I expected. I thought it will get over in a fortnight,' Yuvi replied.

Yuvi realized he shouldn't have said it but he breathed a sigh of relief when Anamika started laughing loudly.

'That is also true. That's a positive way of looking at things,' she continued laughing.

They reached her locality after a few minutes and upon Anamika's insistence, Yuvi stopped the car on the main road itself, a few feet away from her apartment.

Anamika took her coat and was about to get down when Yuvi said, 'Anamika, remember I wanted to tell you something when you were going to Anurag's house?'

Anamika nodded. Soft music played in the background. Anamika's heart was pounding and her palms sweating even in the cold. She had been anxious since the day Yuvi had told her he wanted to say something. She thought the moment had come. She always felt Yuvi would never really make an attempt to share his life with her, maybe because they hadn't spent time alone as she had with Vikrant. This was just the second time Yuvi had shown her how he felt.

'You were going to tell me something,' Anamika reminded him breaking the silence.

'Nothing. It's getting late. You should leave,' Yuvi whispered.

Anamika just smiled and left. Yuvi waved at her and sped away. What did Yuvi want to say? She walked alone on the street towards her apartment. Thinking about her past, she cursed herself for being with Anurag. She kept thinking what the relationship meant to the both of them. Though she had a motive behind the relationship, she was a girl who craved for true love, for appreciation, and for someone to show her the right way. Someone who cared for her and understood her. Anurag was certainly not the one!

She kept walking on the empty street when she heard footsteps behind her. At this hour, normally there is no one walking around. She feared turning back. She kept walking and increased her speed. The footsteps were getting louder.

She was sure there was someone following her. In a fraction of a second, she felt a hand on her shoulder. Her heart skipped a beat. 'Anamika. It's me. I need to talk to you.'

The voice sounded familiar. She turned around and came face to face with her worst nightmare. It was Anurag!

Was he bloody following me for the whole day? Why is he here? Does he want to hurt me? Will he be violent once again?

'Why are you here at this hour? Go away; I don't want to talk to you,' she shouted.

Anurag was hurt, broken and felt betrayed. Every playboy or Casanova needs that one girl in his life who can make him realize what true love is. For Anurag, that girl was Anamika.

'I admit I made a mistake and crossed the boundary with you. I know it's hard for you to forgive me. I insulted you and your self-respect. But I didn't mean to hurt you. I am sorry yet again for causing you pain which was the last thing I ever wanted to do. I don't know what you think about me, but don't you agree that everyone has a past? I hope you listen and see it in my eyes. I am sorry Anamika. I apologize for my mistakes sincerely.'

He went on and on until Anamika interrupted him.

'Look Anurag, Sanaya had told you everything, right? So why are you creating a scene all over again? I know you will get over it easily by dating some other chick who will allow you to do all those things that you wanted in a relationship. Come on, even you know that guys like you can never change.'

The more intimately you are involved with another person, the more difficult it becomes to say I'm sorry. Anurag was certainly involved with Anamika but his treatment was wrong. It is very easy in the heat of the battle to hurt your partner in a very sensitive place. But to repair those wounds is never easy. No wonder Anamika didn't listen to any of his apologies or promises as they all sounded fake. Anurag tried to hug her, kiss her, and get hold of her in every possible way but that didn't work. Anamika didn't want to entertain him anymore and just walked into her apartment. Anurag's ego and his love were shattered one more time. He couldn't take it anymore. It was unbearable for him to get hurt repeatedly by a girl whom he wanted in his life. He texted Anamika before leaving:

'You were the one who took my heart away. But never had I thought you would shred it to pieces. You could have just ripped it in half so that it would be easier to put it back together. But you tore it. Piece by piece, And now, only you can fix it. No one else!'

The next day in college, he kept following her wherever she went. It was so embarrassing for her that she finally screamed in anger and warned him to stay away. Anurag gave up after a long struggle. He tried every way to let her know his feelings but she didn't give a fuck. But he was not the guy who was going to digest her insults with ease. He warned Anamika in front of everyone that he won't let her live happily and would screw her life forever. Anurag was livid with anger.

'Today you've shown me what a liar you are. I thought you were going to stay with me forever, but I was wrong. One day you will be sorry for what you have done. You thought I was going to keep crying like a dejected lover? Yes, I loved you but now you have not only hurt me but my self-respect, my feelings, and my love. You stabbed my heart with a knife, now I will make you suffer, babe. Every time I see your face, it will remind me of how you treated me. I can spread all kinds of rumours about you and spoil your life forever, but I won't do that as you know better what you are. I will make you scream till it hurts. I will push you down and punch you till my knuckles bleed. Whatever I did was because I loved you and because I thought our relationship had reached the next phase. But you left me to die. What did you think? That you were going to make me cry? Bitch, now you will cry! I will tear you down piece by piece just like you tore my heart. You will regret your decision now. Your entire group will.'

He remembered the wonderful moments he had spent with Anamika, the smile which had allured him, those three words which she had said to him. Where had they gone wrong? Now 'I love you' had been replaced with 'Fuck you asshole'.

Music Festival, Delhi University
15th September, 2012

All relationships should come with a precautionary statement: 'Handle with care'. Everything was a mess and things were getting complicated with each passing day. Anamika and Anurag were now back to square one but Anurag was plotting a scheme to take revenge for what she had done to him. Vikrant tried to strike a conversation with Sanaya a couple of times but failed. Yuvi was concentrating on his practice sessions for the upcoming event and told Vikrant and Anamika to do the same. The entire week went in rehearsing for the big event that was coming up. The music festival! VAYU was going to represent Rajhans College and winning the trophy in this event would be a matter of pride for not only VAYU but also for the entire college. This year the event looked bigger, better, and even more promising than the one before. The D day had finally arrived and all of them were ready to give their best knowing the intensity of the event. But none anticipated the disaster that was awaiting them. Just when everything seemed perfect, the mic stopped working and a cord of the electric guitar came apart! Yuvi kept blaming the sound technician for the bizarre set up. No matter how hard the trio tried, things never came back on track. The performance was called off by the judges and the crowd started booing them off. All their hopes were shattered as Yuvi and the other group members walked off the stage with their heads hung in shame. Anamika's sour relationship with her boyfriend had cost them big time! It was probably going to be the last performance of their lives. Rajhans College had lost the competition and the trophy too. Yuvi didn't bother to wait for the results and left with his girlfriend. Vikrant was speechless and didn't know how to react while Anamika feared it was going to be the end of their band VAYU!

Broken Threads

Rajhans College, Delhi
17th September, 2012

What do you call it when all you feel is pain and loneliness? When you are in your house but it doesn't feel like home, when you look back in your life and every choice you made seems wrong, when your loved ones look at you and all you feel is shame, when you smile and laugh but you know it's all fake, and when nothing makes you happy at all. Anamika felt exactly the same. She felt unheard, unseen, depressed, and weak.

'Someone find me, I am scared. Please hold me until it all ends. I don't want to be alone in the dark. Just hold me as I start to disappear from the light. Just hold me so I won't be alone. Do you know what it feels like to be left behind? Losing everyone around you in such little time? I never thought I would cry over someone. I was such a carefree girl before. But now why do I feel as if I'm all alone, as if something is killing me?'

With a heavy heart, she went to college on Monday, the day after the finale performance. She felt as if everyone around her was looking at her and cursing her for what she had done. She wanted to talk to Yuvi and explain to him the entire scenario after apologizing. Yuvi was sitting with Vikrant in a vacant classroom. Anamika felt ashamed to face them and wanted to run away. She wanted her friends back. She went inside the classroom and stood in front of them. Vikrant told her that Yuvi was extremely upset over what had happened yesterday and wanted to be left alone for some time. But Anamika couldn't take it anymore.

'Guys, I am sorry. I never thought Anurag would spoil our show.

'Look Anamika, I had warned you umpteen times that keep your love affairs private and don't let it mess with our performance. But you didn't listen to us. You had to mess with him and spoil everything. How can you even expect us to forgive you? I don't know about Vikrant, but at least I won't forgive you. Vikrant ran away for his true love but you spoiled the show for your own fun. You never wanted a serious relationship and still were roaming around with him. You knew how cheap Anurag is, why did you continue roaming with him? How cheap can you get? Now go and trap another guy. You will gain more popularity.'

'How can you say that? I did not expect this from you. You mean to say I sleep around with guys to increase my popularity? I thought at least you would understand me.

But I was wrong. I never knew you had so much of hatred inside you. '

'Get lost. Don't eat my brains. I beg you to go away right now,' Yuvi screamed.

Anamika had expected at least her friends to understand her. She wanted to hug Yuvi and tell him that it was not her fault. She wanted Yuvi to stand by her and fight against Anurag. But nothing like that happened. Instead Yuvi blamed Anamika. Vikrant told her to leave and assured her not to worry as he would handle the situation. The only person who could convince Yuvi was Vikrant. Anamika left the classroom on Vikrant's suggestion while he tried to calm him down.

A broken piece of thread can never be joined back without a knot. Anamika feared her relationship was headed in the same direction.

'Vikrant! Vikrant!' Anamika came running towards him. Her screams caught him completely off guard.

'They will kill each other. Please, let's go fast.' She caught hold of his hands and lead him towards the main gate.

As they reached the main gate, they saw Yuvi attacking Anurag. Anurag kept defending himself and hitting him back. Yuvi tried to show his dominance by punching him so hard that he fell down to the floor. He tried to get up but Yuvi was in no mood to stop. He kept hitting him hard with the deadliest blows.

Vikrant was speechless and didn't know what to do. Anamika kept screaming and begging for them to stop but they ignored her. Vikrant ran in their direction to put an end to the fight.

'Vikrant, I beg you to please stop them. Please stop,' Anamika kept screaming.

As Vikrant went close, Anurag gave him a strong punch on his stomach that knocked him. This angered Yuvi even more. He pounced on Anurag like a tiger and knocked him to the ground. He could have killed him that moment had Vikrant not interrupted them.

'Yuvi stop it. What are you doing? Don't act childish. Leave him. You've got my swear you will not hit him again,' Yuvi heard a voice behind him say just when he was about to give his final blow. Kashish's words made him stop dead in his tracks. He got up leaving him unconscious on the floor. Blood was rolling down his forehead and the cuts were visible on his face. Even his knuckles were bleeding. If Kashish would not have come there at that moment, a disaster would have happened. Yuvi had completely forgotten that he had called Kashish over since they were supposed to go for a date. Before she could come, Anurag had provoked him, which led to a big fight between the two. He had teased the band's repeated failure and questioned their creditability. Yuvi couldn't digest the insult and had hit him hard.

Kashish dragged him away from the fight scene. Vikrant and Anamika followed them outside the campus. Some of the college staff had watched the act and had already informed the principal about it. Yuvi was given a notice of suspension with immediate effect. It was the end of everything. The end of VAYU.

🔍

Kashish purchased a bottle of Bisleri to clean up Yuvi's wounds. She made him sit near the tapri on the corner of the road. Yuvi hugged her and cried loudly. He was heartbroken. Vikrant and Anamika stood beside them without speaking a word.

'You guys please leave. I don't want him to cry anymore. I can't see him like this. I love him too much,' Kashish pleaded with Vikrant and Anamika.

'Let Vikrant stay. I want him to stay,' Yuvi whispered.

Anamika understood Yuvi didn't want her around. She looked at Kashish who pleaded with her to leave. Anamika felt heartbroken and left. She felt a slight tinge of jealousy that at such critical phase Yuvi had Kashish by his side while she didn't have anyone who could understand her feelings.

'I had told you that her relationship will screw up everything. I had warned you so many times. But no one bothered to hear me or take my words seriously,' Yuvi cried.

'Yuvi forget it. We will get over all this. We will get the band going again. For now, just don't think about it and spoil your health,' Vikrant consoled him by patting his back.

After some time they parted ways. Yuvi and Kashish went to his home by car while Vikrant walked towards the metro station. On his way to the station, Vikrant wondered what life would have been like without Yuvi and Anamika and he realized how important these two friends were to him. He desperately wanted Yuvi and Anamika to re-unite once again. He just prayed that this break up won't lead to the end of their band. Sometimes breaking up can breathe new life and love back into a relationship that has lost its passion and trust. It can act as a wake-up call. When the person we love the most is absent from our lives, we realize how much we truly need them and start valuing them more. Vikrant decided to bring the band back together anyhow. If there was anyone who could, then it was Vikrant. If VAYU had to reunite, Vikrant was the only one who could bring them together. Vikrant knew that even though they showed that they didn't care, nothing could break them apart!

Vikrant boarded the metro and saw Sanaya sitting quietly reading a book. He wondered from which station she had boarded the train as he hadn't seen her at Vishwavidyalaya metro station. He mustered the courage to talk to her.

'Sanaya, I know you don't hate me. It was because of our band that you kept a distance from me. But now you know the bitter truth. I told you that we were in no way connected with Anurag when I approached you for the first time. I also told you that what the reality behind their relationship was. You are ignoring my love for a guy who forced himself on Anamika? What's my fault in it? You think every guy is the same?'

'Vikrant let me tell you clearly. It's not that I hate you. You are a lovely guy. I don't want to take any decision in a hurry. I am not saying that every guy is the same, but my experiences with guys have always been bad. They are all sweet at first. And later, they start taking things for granted; even cheat,' she stated.

She had expressed so openly for the first time in front of Vikrant. She told him many things about Anurag—how he used to abuse her and force himself on her. Vikrant lent her a sympathetic ear. At least it was clear that she didn't hate him and neither was she a wannabe kind of a girl. Vikrant had made the right choice. She would make a perfect wife for him.

'I agree. But ask yourself—do you seriously think that I can hurt you or even harm you? I've been holding my feelings back because I am afraid of its outcome. I don't want you to feel uncomfortable if you don't feel the same way as I do. For a few days, I even tried to get over my feelings but alas! All in vain! You have captivated my heart. I have no work left other than thinking and dreaming about you. You are the most beautiful girl I have ever laid my eyes on. Have you ever seen me talking with any other girl apart from Anamika who is my group member? I am shy to express my feelings because I fear rejection. Whenever I am in a bad mood or am rehearsing for long hours, I think about you and that puts a smile on my face. Think over it. I will always be there for you—whether we remain "just friends" or more. At least don't refuse to take a chance due to that jerk of a guy who doesn't even know what a relationship is. He abused you and insulted you and Anamika and tomorrow it will be someone else. Just get over him. He doesn't deserve so much attention. I will not force you but that's all I wanted to say. Take care.'

Vikrant had poured his heart out to her. Without looking back, he got down at Rajeev Chowk. His honest speech had forced Sanaya to think. She wondered whether Vikrant's feelings were true or was he pretending like Anurag had. Somewhere she felt his feelings were true because of Vikrant's repeated attempts to convince her about his love. Would she be able to accept his love with an open heart or were the grudges of the past going to kill her every minute? Somewhere she felt that he would keep her happy because of his caring nature.

A person's character reflects in his behaviour. Anurag impressed girls by wearing branded clothes and watches, driving luxurious cars, and keeping a heavy bank balance. But what he forgot was that he can't keep the fire in the relationship alive with those brands. To sustain a relationship, you need to pamper a girl with love and care. Vikrant promised to give Sanaya everything she deserved! Sanaya feared those promises would break once more! She could not take another heartbreak.

Dil jab kisike liye sochne pe majboor ho jaaye,
Tab woh dastak hai naye rishte ki shuruvat ki,
Dil jab kisiko aazmaane ke liye qubool kar jaaye,
Tab woh dastak hai naye rishte ki shuruvat ki!!
Dil jab tanhaiyon me kisike liye muskuraane lage,
Tab woh dastak hai naye rishte ki shuruvat ki.
Ahista ahista jab aap kisika yakeen karne lage,
Ahista ahista kisike kareeb jaane lage,
Tab woh dastak hai naye rishte ki shuruvat ki.

Anurag felt cheated and wanted to teach Anamika a lesson. A lesson which she would never forget all her life. His anger had risen to a level that it had become an obsession. For the first time he had loved someone and that girl had betrayed him. The incident with Yuvi acted as a catalyst to fuel his anger. He became furious and made plans to hurt her in such a manner that she could never lead a normal life again. He had started drinking regularly to avoid the pain. Sometimes he even slept in his car or on the pavement outside the bar—not knowing what he was thinking and speaking. On one such day, he messaged Anamika,

You told me that no one could ever replace me. You lied!
You told me that I was your one and only. You lied! You told
me that you would love me forever and never let me go. You
lied! You told me that you would forgive and forget about

everything I did wrong. You lied! You told me that you will erase the memories of that night. You lied! You told me that you will never leave me. You lied! You told me you would never lie to me! YOU LIED! All you did was lie and cheat. Just get out of my sight, get out of my mind. Get out of this world. This feeling in my chest is no longer just a feeling. You held my hand when you needed me and threw me away after using me. Now when I want you, you slapped my love. I will kill you. You won't live happily ever. This is just a start. Your band is over, and now me teri band bajaunga. Fuck off.

Anamika didn't pay attention to his threat messages. She had decided she was not going to let his anger affect her. She wanted to lead a life of normalcy again. She even changed her mobile number and decided to block him on WhatsApp. But he caught hold of her number from somewhere and started calling her up again. In every message and phone call he just warned her that if she did not forgive him, he will make her regret one day and even harm her. Anamika was a brave girl and handled it on her own without letting anyone know except Vikrant as he was the only true friend she could trust. Yuvi had been keeping a distance from her ever since that incident. Their distance increased as the days passed. It was getting difficult for Vikrant to handle both Yuvi and Anamika. He cared for both, he loved them both, and wanted them together. But life is strange. It always does the opposite of what you want.

Mia Bella
15th September, 2013, Around 5 am

'I can't believe it. Shit man, how could he even think like that,' Sakshi wondered aloud.

'No one could believe what was happening at that time. But it was the truth. Everything was slipping from our hands. The band, fame, friendship, love, and grades. In short, our life had come to a standstill and we had no control over it,' Vikrant stated.

I had no words to describe my emotions. I admired the courage Vikrant had showed in narrating the story to us. You don't realize how strong a person really is until you see them in their weakest moment.

He had narrated the entire story to us even though it was hard for him to think about it again. If you look up the meaning of 'friend' in the dictionary, you will find that friend means a person with whom one has a bond of mutual affection who guides us through loss and pain. He had tried to be such a friend to Yuvi and Anamika. But when a bond is broken, is there any hope for a reunion? When words have different meanings, when feelings are left ignored, is there any hope for a reunion? Maybe our misguided actions are a part of our lives that enable us to learn from them and fully discover ourselves.

A few misconstrued words and misguided actions had put their friendship in risk. What was more surprising for me was to see how nasty Anurag could get. He was ready to even kill Anamika for the sake of revenge! And then he said he loved her. I still felt the same and believed it was the after effect of the break-up.

'Did Anurag and Anamika come face to face with each other again? How did Anamika react to those messages? I mean, she should have filed a complaint against him straight away,' I said.

'I told her the same thing. But she didn't want her parents to get into any trouble. I was worried for her, as I knew how vicious Anurag was. His friends said that he has changed and seriously loved Anamika and wanted her back in his life but that was not the way to win someone's love. Every day I feared for Anamika when she left the college premises alone. But she preferred to not tell the cops about it. You know how tough it gets for a girl, right? I mean the cops will ask all kind of weird questions to her in front of her family. She was brave enough to handle it on her own so she decided to simply ignore him. However, Anurag never tried to follow her home or harass her physically. Whatever he did was through text messages and calls.'

'What about Yuvi?' Sakshi inquired.

'What about him?' Vikrant said sipping his drink.

'I mean what about the grudges that had developed between Yuvi and Anamika?' she said reframing her query.

'It was unbearable for me. Every day I tried some or the other way to bring them close but that didn't help. They kept avoiding each other for silly reasons. Anamika had no issues but Yuvi had many. He was upset obviously upset because of their performance at the intercollege festival for which he blamed Anamika. But he was more upset because of the love that viewers showered on Anamika. Wherever we went to perform, guys and girls would go crazy for Anamika and that brought a sense of insecurity in Yuvi. He was the lead and wanted more appreciation but that didn't happen. Not because he lagged somewhere in his performance but because Anamika was the more popular of the two because of her hot looks. It killed Yuvi from within and made him behave badly with Anamika.'

'Was he even attracted to her? That's what you said,' I asked.

'Yes, the fact was that the more he tried to hate her, the more he got attracted to her. Rather obsessed with her. He never told anyone about it though. Kashish was the one rescuing factor in his life. Had she not been present with him in his difficult hour, he would have gone insane,' Vikrant explained.

Some moments bring us together, some moments tear us apart, and some moments change us forever! That evening had changed Yuvi forever.

'Did you manage to bring them together?' Sakshi asked curiously.

'Yuvi was hurt. Bringing them together as they were before was a tough task. Yuvi had lost everything except Kashish. He suspension letter came as a shock for him and changed everything. Things slowly took a turn for the worse. I kept telling him that we had to reunite for the band's sake and that things were finally shaping up for the better. That trip was the last chance to bring them together.'

'What does that mean?' I asked immediately.

'I convinced Yuvi and Anamika to come along for a trip with me and my love. They had no choice but to say yes. I had hit bull's eye. The trip was my way of bringing them together,' Vikrant smiled.

'What are you saying? I can't understand anything Vikrant,' I said scratching my head.

'When I met Sanaya in the metro that day, she was forced to think about what I had said. I had told Yuvi to convince Sanaya to join us for an overnight trip. She thought of Yuvi as a friend and trusted him. By taking her on the trip, I wanted an opportunity to show my real self that she was not acquainted with. Life seemed like a struggle, but there was one thing that remained constant. My love for Sanaya. My love had no definition. Yuvi knew how much I wanted Sanaya in my life though she was senior to me. Yuvi had agreed to convince Sanaya. He was on talking terms with her and it was not difficult for him to convince her as they both had one thing in common. Hatred for Anurag. Every time he would meet her, he would start praising me in front of her. In due course of time, he was able to convince her to come for the trip. Though she was not on talking terms with me or Anamika, she agreed to come for Yuvi's sake. He also told me that she had a soft corner for me and I just need to make the most of this trip and tell her all I had in my heart. Yuvi had already created a good image of me in front of her. All that was needed was a push,' Vikrant explained.

It was the beginning of a new relationship. Vikrant was positive that this trip would bring all of them together. Sometimes the best beginnings of our lives may end in sorrow but sometimes even after darkest days, the sun shines brightly the next day. Vikrant hoped for the sun to shine bright, bringing a ray of hope to their lives.

The story had completely taken over me. I had gone through so much in my life. But after listening to their story, I realized so many people in the world are sailing in the same boat as me. I was living their lives listening to Vikrant and experiencing all the pain that they had gone through. At a difficult junction in their lives, Vikrant had donned the cap of leader and was managing the troop well. He had brought Yuvi, Anamika and Sanaya together which was certainly no small feat. He knew exactly what he was doing. The only time he did not know what to do was when he came face to face with Sanaya. But that's love and we should love a girl like the last drop of alcohol in a bottle on a dry day.

'So what happened next? Where did you all decide to go?' I was curious to know more.

'We were yet to decide the place. I wanted to leave the decision to Yuvi, Anamika, and Sanaya so that they could get talking each other while planning for the trip. I preferred to isolate myself from the planning just for the sake of our friendship. Even small discussions can help to bring back that intimacy in a broken friendship. More importantly, I wanted Anamika and Sanaya to gel well together. Both were equally important people of my life. I was somewhat successful in getting things right by bringing them under one roof. At least they didn't throw things at each other. They even smiled occasionally and as the day of the trip came closer, the frequency of smiles increased between them. We had decided to go to Daman.'

'Did Sanaya get any hint that was going to happen there?'

'Yes. She had a hint that I was planning to propose to her. That encouraged me more. Even though she knew about my plans, she seemed perfectly normal. Was Yuvi behind it? I had no idea whatsoever. I didn't dig for the reason behind it as I was content at least they were getting along well with each other,' Vikrant replied.

It was a new start to things. Relationships are like lemons, sweet and sour. Vikrant and Sanaya were scared to show their feelings because of their past experiences. But Vikrant never gave up trying. He never let go even though Sanaya said she was not ready for it. As days went by, they realized that this feeling inside them cannot be denied anymore. Sanaya made him fall crazily in love with her.

Feelings always speak the truth. If you try to hide them, then they come out through other unspoken means like body language and facial expressions. And when you are in love, it's never too late. I sat back and relaxed. I wanted to hear more. Yuvi-Kashish and now Vikrant-Sanaya's relationship made me realize that two relationships can never be the same. There are different thoughts, feelings, and people involved.

'Kashish didn't join you all?' Sakshi asked.

'No, she had a family function to attend that week. But we all were ready to have fun, including Yuvi. I was nervous as I had to express my love to Sanaya and make her feel special. I wanted to let her know how much I loved her and needed her in my life. Our journey started on 2nd October and we reached Vapi a day later by the Aug-Kranti Express.'

The Way You Make Me Feel

Daman district, Daman & Diu
3rd October, 2012

It's hard to let go of the past, especially when it's witness to the best memories of your life. Vikrant wanted to bring back those old days—the time when they would sit in the college compound for hours doing nothing except checking out beautiful girls and handsome boys. He wanted to bring back those moments when they would get drunk and scream on the roads of Delhi at midnight. When they did long rehearsals in college and forgot they had to take a class test the next morning. When they bunked a few lectures to run after hot girls in short dresses. Anamika, just to bring back their attention, would come wearing an even shorter one the next day. They had experienced the time of their lives and it wasn't easy for them to forget about it. We can easily erase such memories from our mind but our heart doesn't allow it. Though Vikrant had managed to convince both of them to go for a holiday trip, he was not able to find a way to get them to talk. They had reached Vapi by train from Delhi and had taken a taxi to Daman. All through the way, Yuvi and Anamika exchanged a few smiles but didn't interact much. Vikrant and Sanaya didn't have to say anything to each other. Their eyes spoke a million words. Yuvi had bettered Vikrant's image in front of Sanaya and she was slowly coming around to liking him. After a very long time, Sanaya had felt attracted to another man.

'Vikrant, which hotel are we staying in?' Sanaya enquired.

'The Chill Out Resort,' Vikrant answered. He had planned the entire trip as he had been to Daman before and was familiar with the place.

'Have you booked three rooms?' Yuvi asked.

'Why?' Vikrant was puzzled.

'You and Sanaya will be in one room, right? I thought you both will chill out together in your Chill Out Resort. So we will require three rooms, right?' Yuvi was in a mood to tease Vikrant.

'Shut up you…'

'Yuvi, even I don't mind taking three rooms. But you will stay alone, poor boy?' Sanaya teased further.

'He will be daydreaming about Kashish and the time they have spent together. If you don't miss her, I will give you company,' Vikrant laughed and the others followed. 'Ewwww!!' said Yuvi in reaction to Vikrant's suggestion. He squeezed Vikrant's nipples hard and said 'Chota chota pungi'.

'Yaar, how many times have I told you not to do this. It hurts. What the fuck do you get by doing this?' Vikrant shouted. Everyone laughed in unison.

They had a fun time all the way to the resort. They reached the resort within an hour and got down from the taxi.

'What have you told your parents?' Sanaya asked.

'We all have told our parents that we are going on a college trip organized by the student council,' Anamika answered.

'Oh God, you guys are impossible. You should have told the truth instead,' she muttered.

'Yes, I agree with you. I should have told my parents that I am going with Vikrant and two other girls who happens to be our friend. Both the guys will stay in one room and the girls will be in another room. Dad please don't misunderstand us as we won't smoke or drink. We are just going to have a good time with our friends,' Yuvi said in a sarcastic way.

Sanaya started laughing. Yuvi always had her in splits. They wanted some thrill in their lives and here it was. Not that their parents wouldn't have allowed them to go, but they wanted to relax, have fun, and enjoy a true beach holiday away from the worries of daily life. The resort was a nice place to stay and everyone appreciated Vikrant for choosing such a pleasant place to chill.

'If simplicity is the essence of beauty, then this resort is it,' Sanaya said while walking inside the resort.

It had a delightful dining area called 'Verandah'. They were looking forward to relaxing in the pool area and fresh lemon sodas in hand.

'This is amazing. We are going to fucking enjoy our holiday by drinking, dancing, smoking,' said Yuvi in excitement. 'Do we get a nice massage here like we did in Goa?'

'Oh darling, let's check in. Stop living in your own little fantasy world. Do you want me to call Kashish and tell her that her boyfriend needs a massage,' Sanaya teased.

'Vikrant, please explain to her how it feels to get a massage from a sexy girl who is not your girlfriend. Those smooth relaxing hands moving gently on your shoulder and back, taking you to higher levels of ecstasy,' Yuvi explained.

'You mean even Vikrant?' Sanaya asked.

'Oh crap! I don't do such things. Sanaya don't listen to him. He is trying to…' Vikrant interrupted.

'Trying to what? Speak up. Come on dude,' Yuvi teased.

Vikrant kicked his ass and pushed him inside the room.

'Sach bolne ka ye inaam milta hai. Sanaya, I am warning you,' Yuvi shouted jumping on the bed in his room.

Vikrant and Sanaya knew that Yuvi was just pulling their leg and having fun. They finally seemed to be coming closer to each other. Vikrant remembered the first time he had seen Sanaya in the metro. He had never thought they would be together ever. She sat there so innocently and her beauty was such a delight to his eyes. Everything had changed since then. Vikrant could clearly see the love for him in her eyes.

It was the beginning of their love story. New love is like a brand new car which you can't wait to go on a long drive in. It's like a secret shared over a romantic dinner.

Some people walk into our lives by accident and stay with us in our hearts forever!

'Don't take Yuvi so seriously. He loves to provoke others,' Vikrant said to Sanaya as they walked together near the poolside after settling down in their respective rooms.

'It's okay. I know his intentions weren't bad.' Sanaya blushed looking at Vikrant.

Walking along the poolside on a sunny day with your love can put your hormones out of whack. They had a strong desire to hold each other's hands and gaze into each other's eyes. After their short walk, Vikrant and Sanaya decided to have one drink together. They both ordered fresh lime sodas and sat with their feet immersed in the pool. The waiter came in with their drinks a few minutes later. He kept the drinks on a tray beside them and left.

'Here you go,' Vikrant said handing her the drink.

'Thanks,' she replied.

Their conversation was way too formal and both were waiting for the other to make the first move. Vikrant was nervous but he had to proceed, as Sanaya was the main reason why he had planned this trip besides bringing Yuvi and Anamika's friendship back to normal. Yuvi had laid the foundation stone by bringing Vikrant and Sanaya together. Now it was Vikrant's turn to take it forward.

'I hope you are over Anurag. He is certainly not your type of guy,' Vikrant spoke.

Oh God! Doesn't he know that one should not talk about a girl's past affairs, especially when you want to take a step forward in the relationship, Sanaya thought to herself and smiled.

Shit shit! I shouldn't have talked about Anurag. Vikrant, you are such a fool. Fuck yourself now. He knew he had made a mistake.

'Sanaya, you deserve a guy who will take care of you, pamper you, and protect you from all the troubles that come your way. He should not allow even a single scratch on your body or even a tear in your eyes. I am not overdoing it, but just showing you a mirror. A mirror which reflects not only your image on it but also your soul.'

'How do you know what kind of a guy I want?' she blushed.

'That's what my heart said. The first time I saw you, I felt that any guy you marry will be the luckiest guy in the world. The innocent smile on your face reflects your simplicity.'

'Really?' Sanaya questioned in excitement.

She had never felt like this before. Anurag had never pampered her in their one-year relationship and she did not know the real meaning of love and togetherness. He had always been violent with her. She was thus afraid of relationships and did not want anyone in her life. But ever since she met Vikrant, everything seemed new to her. The love and attention that Vikrant gave her was something she not only liked but wanted desperately in her life. She was so lost in that small conversation with Vikrant that she forgot to notice Yuvi and Anamika were standing right there behind them listening to their conversation.

'Yes, really. You make my world go round. My princess, I want you to be with me forever,' Yuvi said on behalf of Vikrant.

'Even I want to be with you forever. Please be my hero. My dabangg,' Anamika replied on behalf of Sanaya.

'You bastard. You fucking idiot. You asshole…'

Vikrant hurled abuses at Yuvi with all the possible slang words he knew for interrupting his conversation with Sanaya at such a critical juncture. Anamika couldn't control her laughter and fell down rolling on floor. Sanaya was red in the face out of embarassment.

It's said that you can find love in the most unexpected places. But who would have thought that Vikrant would find love in the Delhi Metro. A guy who really loves his girlfriend is not the one who will get cozy in public but the one who will tell her, 'You deserve to be respected'. Vikrant was one such guy who treated Sanaya like his princess.

Sanaya had repeatedly ignored Vikrant and kept lusting after Anurag even though he was not meant for her. She had hurt Vikrant's sentiments and had kept crying for Anurag. But the past few days had changed her perception towards love and Vikrant. She would run away from relationships after her break up because of the trauma she had undergone. But Vikrant had entered her life and had become her guardian angel. Before she met him, there was emptiness in her life that threatened to break her completely. However, Vikran't mere presence put the smile back on her face. She was enjoying every sweet moment with him and the band VAYU. He had introduced vibrant colors to her boring, grey life. Isn't it ironic that we ignore those who adore us and adore those who ignore us? We hurt those who love us and love those who hurt us.

Devka Beach, Daman

'This is not fair. You both are making us run for some drops of water,' Yuvi shouted as he came running towards the shore.

'Run, Yuvi, run. Otherwise get ready to lose,' Anamika screamed.

They were playing 'Water Relay', in which Yuvi and Vikrant were made to run to the sea, fill a small cup of water, and run back to dump it into the cup which Anamika and Sanaya were holding on their heads. All of them were having a ball at Devka beach, one of Daman's most famous beaches which is well known for its vast stretches of sand. The beaches are often quite deserted. They could hear the mighty waves crashing against the rocks. Vikrant tried different tricks to get Anamika and Yuvi to talk like before. He paired up Yuvi with Anamika in the game so that they could be together as a team and talk. The plan worked somehow as after every round they interacted casually with each other like they used to do earlier. They even had smiles on their faces.

'Vikrant, we have to win anyhow. Don't spill the cup of water.' It was Sanaya this time who laughed as Vikrant came running towards her.

The losing team had to foot the bill of the dinner that night. Eventually Yuvi lost the game badly losing five out of eight rounds. Vikrant was happy not because he won, but because he had succeeded in getting Yuvi and Anamika to talk to each other.

'Freak, you gave me a small cup. I'm sure,' said Yuvi defending his loss.

'Don't cry like a kid after losing. Be ready to empty your pockets tonight. It's going to be one hell of a night. I am going to drink like there's no tomorrow,' Vikrant said in excitement.

They both gave each other a tough look and then busted out in laughter. Friendship is one factor that makes our life worthwhile. When you have a friend to confide in, suffering seems more bearable, and pleasures become more intense. Everything is better when you have a friend to share your feelings with. When friendship breaks, there is a degree of pain and sorrow that we all go through because you feel a void in your life. Yuvi and Anamika too had gone through the same thing. Vikrant's continuous efforts had brought them together and they finally shared a hug after the game. There were smiles all over.

'Tell me who enjoys the beach most?' Yuvi asked as they walked towards the ice-cream shop.

'Couples?' Anamika answered.

'Naah.'

'Kids?' she answered once more.

'Nope. No one else enjoys the beach more than the lifeguard on duty. Not because of the warmth of the sun or the beauty of the night but because of all the babes they get to watch over. All the babes who come to the beach in their tight sexy swimsuits. He is the king of the beach,' Yuvi said.

'Yuvi, when will you change?' Vikrant asked.

'When you will get married. As of now let me be myself.'

After eating ice-cream, Vikrant and Sanaya went for a walk on the shore alone . Anamika and Yuvi sat on the shore gazing at the waves and watching the sun go down.

'Are you still angry with me?' Anamika whispered in Yuvi's ears.

'Not really. I was upset with whatever happened and it had hurt me badly,' he said picking up a pebble and throwing it in the ocean.

'Do you really think it was my fault? I never wanted that to happen. I didn't have the slightest clue that something like that had been planned by Anurag. Vikrant must have told you how he tried to force himself on me. He abused me too.'

'I think you shouldn't have been with him in the first place. But before coming here for a holiday, Kashish made me understand how you must have felt that time which changed my perception. I've never told you this, but when I thought about it I felt like you were not wrong.'

'What did she say?' Anamika asked in curiosity.

'Kashish made me understand how a girl feels when she is under the threat of not only getting ragged by seniors but also by those who pass weird comments whenever she walks alone. She made me understand why you must have taken that decision of being with him. I appreciate the fact that despite being with him, you never did anything wrong. Vikrant told me whatever had happened that night at Anurag's place was totally his fault. His behaviour was equally responsible for that big fight in college which resulted in my suspension.'

'I am extremely sorry for that. I was feeling so guilty that because of me…' Anamika couldn't control her tears.

Yuvi interrupted her and consoled her that it was not her fault. He told her that even he had made the mistake of doubting her. They hugged each other and apologized for letting their misconceptions come in the way of their friendship. But Yuvi still didn't understand why was he attracted towards her. He felt a current running in his body after that hug. There's a reason behind every new person's entry in your life. You may not know it then, but one day you figure out why. Yuvi was yet to figure out why he was attracted towards her even though Kashish was the love of his life and they had been together for four long years. Some relationships were turning complicated while some were establishing a strong foundation of love!

The Closer I Get to You

Chill Out Resort, Daman

When we really love someone, we can never be 'just friends'. It's never easy to hide your emotions within you and keep the friendship alive. Vikrant never wanted Sanaya and him to be just friends. But Sanaya did not want to be in another relationship due to her past experiences. She was not sure if her heart was ready to be loved again, to have someone again in her life.

Vikrant and Sanaya were sitting on the couch in the veranda of the resort spending some alone time together. Yuvi and Anamika had left them alone on purpose so that the motive behind the trip gets solved. As they sat together chit-chatting about their families and friends, Vikrant came closer to her and said,

'Sanaya, can I share something with you?'

Vikrant's closeness made her cautious but secretly she was loving it.

'I have always dreamt of a girl who would not only understand me but also my family. She would support me through my bad times and share my joy in good times. I want her to accept me as I am. I am a family-oriented guy. I may have very few friends, but I know the ones I have will be with me whenever I need them. I want my girl to respect them and my loved ones. Obviously, even I will understand her feelings and take care of her needs...'

Sanaya interrupted him and said, 'Vikrant I know you are a very nice person and that you will pamper your girlfriend. But I have been through so much in my life that sometimes I fear what if same things repeat once again. I trust you as a person.'

Sanaya couldn't hide the love in her eyes. The only thing which made her worry was painful memories of Anurag.

'Do you know that I am younger to you?' Vikrant asked with a smile on his face.

'I know but that's fine,' she muttered without thinking.

Her smile had erased all the doubts he had in his mind. He could see the burning desire for him in her eyes. Vikrant just wanted to be with her, to gently touch her face and look into her beautiful eyes. He wanted to lie next to her, rub her back as they talked about their feelings for one another. He wanted her to know how much he cherished and adored her. His heart longed for her love, to feel the passion as he caressed her face and kissed her, to see their love for one another grow. Though he was younger to her, he never saw it as a hindrance. Sanaya's expression also showed that she did not see the age difference as a problem. She was slowly coming around the fact that he was the one for her. She realized that she was never in love with Anurag in the truest sense of the word. What she had misunderstood as love was mere infatuation. We get so used to a person that we start mistaking the dependence as love. But when someone enters your life and introduces you to true love, you realize you were never in love before. To truly love someone, one has to follow certain key principles. Vikrant had all of these: admiration, adoration, appreciation, assurance, desire, fondness, giving undivided attention, loyalty, passion, respect, understanding, and the first and foremost, love!

Vikrant sent a WhatsApp message to Yuvi saying,

I think it's the right moment for me to tell her what I feel and how much I love her. I hope tonight my relationship status will change from single to committed.

Yuvi wished him good luck. He looked towards Sanaya and said, 'Sanaya, let's go to the beach. Just you and me. Only if you don't mind.'

He tried to be modest though he knew that Sanaya was not going to say no.

'Anything special?' she smiled.

'Nothing really. Just that I was getting bored here and need some fresh air,' Vikrant added.

She was clearly as nervous as him. Sanaya knew that the moment was here and it made her anxious. When she had met Vikrant the first time, she hadn't realized he would make her fall in love with him. She had no plans on getting attracted to someone but he had awakened in her those feelings she had forgotten existed.

Devka beach, Daman

Love is a strange feeling. It gives you strength and hope that nothing can go wrong. Vikrant and Sanaya had gone through a storm of emotions but cupid had managed to successfully bring them together. When you stop believing in love because of a broken heart, it's often hard to start over. However, when you meet someone who tugs at your heartstrings and knows you better than yourself, you have no choice but to give in. Sanaya had all kinds of thoughts running through her mind. Was what she had experienced earlier with Anurag love or was what she facing now with Vikrant love? Before she had met him, everything was a mess and her life was in complete shatters. Vikrant entered her life and within a few days things changed everything.

They walked towards the deserted area on the sea shore where there were no people.

'Why have we come here? It's so scary,' Sanaya whispered.

'Sssh. Relax. I am not going to hurt you. Don't worry,' said Vikrant keeping his finger on her lips.

His touch sent her to heaven. It was for the first time he had touched her. What followed was a long pause between the two. Sanaya couldn't hold herself anymore and slowly planted a small kiss on his lips. She smiled shyly and closed her eyes. Vikrant felt goosebumps all over his body. He had waited for this moment forever.

He held her hands and said, 'I have something for you. I don't know how you will react but I just couldn't prolong it any further.'

Saying this he went behind the rocks. Sanaya couldn't see what Vikrant was doing exactly but could sense that he was picking up something from behind the rocks. Sanaya was confused and looked around. There was nobody in sight. After a few seconds, he returned with a balloon stuffed with rose petals. She didn't know about it then, but one of the balloons also had a ring placed inside it. He came close to her and burst the balloons over her head. All the petals came showering down. He came closer to her and slowly whispered in her ears,

'You will never forget this moment. Will you be my better half?'

Sanaya was speechless. Nobody had made her feel so special before. She pinched herself to make sure it wasn't a dream. She looked away in embarrassment. Vikrant turned her to face him. He went closer to her and nervously held her hand. Sanaya couldn't look into his eyes as she was so nervous. She looked down and saw a note which had fallen from one of the balloons. She opened it and read,

I don't know where to start with you. The first time I saw your innocent face in the metro, I started dreaming about our future together. You took all my pain, suffering, and hurt away.

I don't know how to explain it to you. I see a future with you. I want you to be my wife and mother to our kids. I can spend my entire life telling you how much I love you. I thank God each day for introducing me to such an amazing girl. You are the girl who I can take to my parents and proudly say, 'This is my choice'. You have everything I look for in my dream girl and no one can break our bond ever.

All I know at this point is that if this is right, it won't go away so easily. Our bond will keep getting stronger. Both of us are carrying baggage from our pasts. But we don't have to let it cause problems in our present. We will work through it. Trust me, my love, I will always stand by your side in your bad times. I want to be yours forever. Let's live our lives the way we deserve to live it.

Tere bina tutkar bikhar jayenge,
Tum mil gaye to gulshan ki tarah khil jayenge,
Tum na mile to jite ji mar jayenge,
Tumhe paa liya to markar bhi jee jayenge...

Sanaya was dumbstruck. She had never believed someone could love her so much. Certainly not after the Anurag episode. She was not over him completely, but she couldn't stop herself from coming close to Vikrant. What she felt around her happened only in movies and not in real life. The more she had tried to run away from this feeling, the more she had come closer to him. Every moment and every incident made her believe that she deserved to be loved and that Vikrant was the right person for it. She had two choices in front of her. Either take a risk and accept his proposal hoping for a better future or reject it and regret it for the rest of her life. She made up her mind and ran into his arms, hugging him as tightly as she could.

'I love you,' she whispered.

'What did you say? Say it again,' said Vikrant breaking the hug and gazing at her.

'I said, I love you.'

'Can you repeat that again?'

'I love you,' she repeated it once again.

Vikrant hugged her tightly as if there was no tomorrow. It was beginning of a new life for them!

'I want you to keep saying it over and over again. I love you so much. How desperately I have waited to hear this from you. Today I feel complete,' Vikrant said holding her face in his hands.

He made her lean against the rock and placed his arms around her waist. He stroked her back as he leant in for a sweet kiss, his lips touching hers. He tried to open her mouth seductively with his tongue. To tease him, she resisted at first, but slowly let him in. He thrust his tongue inside her mouth and explored it with a burning desire. By the end of it, they were exhausted and out of breath. With a broad smile on her face, Sanaya again kissed him gently.

She was about to give up on life when Yuvi introduced her to Vikrant. It was not easy for her to accept another man's proposal, but she couldn't say no to Vikrant. She had mentally prepared herself for this decision. When she agreed to come along for the Daman trip, somewhere in the corner of her mind she knew that Vikrant would surely propose. From that day itself, she was trying hard to stay away from him to test herself if she could actually stay away. But she failed miserably! She gave up and accepted the fact that even she loved Vikrant. Resting in his arms, she felt content. Vikrant had given her the much needed warmth in her life.

Out of nowhere, Yuvi and Anamika pounced on them and popped the remaining balloon which had the ring in it. The rose petals came falling down on them and they broke their kiss. Yuvi caught hold of the ring in time.

Vikrant was about to hit Yuvi when all of a sudden, Yuvi started singing, '*Waah waah raamji, jodi kya banaayi, Bhaiya aur Bhabi ko badhaai ho badhaai…*'

'Yuvi what the hell are you doing here?' Vikrant shouted.

Vikrant had told Yuvi and Anamika to keep the balloons behind the rock a few minutes before they reach and leave the place once they arrive. But both of them hadn't left and had watched the entire scene unfold before them. This annoyed Vikrant. It was their first kiss and he had wanted it to be special with no one around. Yuvi had proved that 'Har ek friend kamina hota hai'. Yuvi had made a bakra of him!

'*Suno jijaji, aji aap ke liye, meri jiji ne bade tap hai kiye, mandiron mein kiye phere, pooja saanjh savere, teen lok, tain tees devon ko yeh rahi ghere…*' Anamika continued taking Sanaya's case.

'Jaisi maine maangi thi, vaisi bhabhi paayi, Jiji aur jija ko badhaai ho badhaai…'

By planning to bring Vikrant and Anamika close, even Yuvi and Anamika had forgotten their differences. Earlier, Vikrant had doubted whether Sanaya loved him or not. Sanaya thought that her actions showed love but actions are often misconstrued. His heart needed an assurance that she truly loved him and he needed to hear those actual words, *'I love you'*, from her. She had said those words today and given a go-ahead to their relationship. He had offered her a shoulder to cry on, arms to be held safe in, hands to hold for as long as she wished, and a special place in his life that no one could fill in. They hugged each other again after Vikrant placed the ring on Sanaya's finger. They headed back towards the resort as it was party time! Yuvi had decided to throw a party not only because he had lost the water game in the morning but also because his friend was now committed. Sanaya still couldn't hide her emotions and kept blushing all through the way to resort. She was deeply in love with Vikrant. Anamika too was happy for both of them. Looking at them, she longed for someone with whom she could share her feelings. She was hurt and all alone. Vikrant felt victorious as he had completed his mission. The motive behind his trip had been accomplished. Vikrant and Sanaya were going to begin a new innings of their life and VAYU had once again come together!

Not All Nights are Romantic

Chill Out Resort, Daman

Many people say they want to find true love, even when it's right in front of them. They're either blind to it, take it for granted, or throw it away. It's better to take a chance rather than regret something your whole life. Sanaya had taken her own time to convince herself that she was in love.

'Be with me always. I need you all my life, baby,' Vikrant whispered in her ear and kissed it gently.

She made him sit down on the sofa and looked deep into his eyes. Then she took her hand in his and said,

'You are not my first love, but you are my best love. I am not going anywhere baby and I love you so much. I want to hold you in my arms, kiss you whenever I want, lay in bed with you for hours, and just be there by your side. I never thought someone would love me so much. I promise I will be with you always.'

Both of them had left behind the baggage of their past and had decided to shift into the same room at the hotel. The joke about booking three rooms had actually come true. They wanted to make their first night memorable. Sanaya was ready to melt in his arms that night as she knew Vikrant would never hurt her and would never break her trust. But she was still afraid to cross her limits. They were sitting in Vikrant and Yuvi's room till the luggage was shifted to their room by housekeeping.

'Oh honeymoon couples, don't forget to join us for the party in a few minutes. I don't want you putting a "Do not disturb" tag on the door and locking it when I come knocking,' Yuvi teased them.

'Shut up Yuvi,' protested Sanaya throwing the AC remote-control at him. He escaped being hit by ducking at the right moment.

Once the luggage was shifted, Vikrant took her in the other room and they both lay on the bed looking into each other's eyes.

'I don't want to go back to Delhi. I want to stay here with you. I want to spend my days and my nights with you. Please, let's not go back.'

Vikrant nodded in agreement to make her happy. He didn't want to spoil the moment. With every hug, their heart showered petals of love on them. With every kiss, their heart showered petals of trust on them. With every gaze, their heart showered petals of togetherness on them, and with every passionate moment, their heart showered petals of romance on them. They had a cosy cuddling session before Yuvi came knocking on the door. Sanaya rushed to freshen up.

'Come in,' Vikrant shouted.

Yuvi came in and told them to get ready as soon as possible.

'Come on dude. You have the whole night to romance. Get ready otherwise we will not be able to enjoy ourselves and make the most of the night. I am going down to look at the menu and order drinks. Till then you freshen up and come down to the Veranda lounge. It has a wonderful ambience. Come soon,' Yuvi said and left the room.

Sanaya came out with a towel wrapped around her body. Her hair were wet and water drops trickled down her body. Vikrant gave her a wink and asked her to come close to him. Sanaya pinched him hard and told him to control his feelings.

'Vikrant, you better stop looking at me like this. Will you tell me what I should wear?' Sanaya said showing him a couple of tops and shorts she had brought along with her for the trip.

Vikrant told her to wear a blue top—as that was his favourite colour—with black cotton shorts.

'Shut your eyes while I change,' Sanaya said with a shy smile.

'It's okay. I will look the other way,' Vikrant smiled.

'No. Don't act smart. Shut your eyes and open them only when I tell you to,' Sanaya ordered.

Vikrant followed her orders and kept his hands on his eyes till Sanaya changed her clothes. He knew she was merely teasing him by not allowing him to take a quick peak.

'Vikrant, I want to tell you something,' she said once she was done dressing. 'I don't want us to have sex before marriage. I am okay with getting cozy, but to a limit.'

Vikrant smiled and told her that he had no issues with it as his love was not restricted to physical attraction alone. He loved her mentally and emotionally as well. He knew her fears about getting physical stemmed from her painful past experiences with Anurag. Remembering those moments still made her shiver and gave her nightmares. She was not completely over it as the pain was so deep that it was not easy for her to forget everything in such a short span of time. Vikrant was aware of this fact because Yuvi had given him a hint about it.

'Baby, I am not with you for sex alone. I love you for what you are. I want your support. You are my mental support. Your presence gives me a sense of security Don't worry at all as such things won't harm our relationship. I love you,' Vikrant said kissing her.

'I love you too.'

'Come on now, we are getting late. Yuvi and Anamika will be waiting for us downstairs at the lounge.' Vikrant locked the door of their room and led her to the lounge.

Time decides whom you meet in life, your heart decides whom you want in your life, but your behaviour decides who will stay in your life. Who knew Vikrant and Sanaya would go from being complete strangers to being in a relationship in such a short amount of time? Some things are so unpredictable.

'Why have you come here alone? Where is Anamika?' Vikrant questioned Yuvi taking the chair next to him at the bar counter. Sanaya also took a seat beside Vikrant.

'She has a severe headache and told me to tell you guys that she will join us in some time,' Yuvi replied. He called out to the bartender and ordered drinks for them.

'What will you drink?' Yuvi asked Sanaya.

'No, you guys carry on.'

'Let's wait for Anamika then. What say? We should celebrate the reunion of VAYU,' Vikrant suggested. He was expecting both of them to give him a positive nod.

'Dude, don't be so formal. We will celebrate our reunion once she comes. Till then let's celebrate your union. Cheers!' Yuvi smiled raising a toast to Vikrant and Sanaya.

Before coming to the lounge, Yuvi had doped alone in his hotel room and was carrying marijuana for Vikrant too. Vikrant looked towards Sanaya for permission and asked her if she was okay with it. Sanaya didn't say anything. He realized Sanaya wasn't too happy about it, so he politely refused Yuvi's offer. He didn't want to go against her wishes and put her off. After all, it was their first night together.

The lounge had a very romantic ambience. The bar was stocked with every imported brand one could ask for. The musical fountain in the middle of the lounge which changed its colour according to the beats of the music was also an added attraction for visiting tourists. The trance music being played took them to a different world. Sanaya requested Yuvi to sing their theme song for Vikrant and herself. But they had a different plan in mind.

'So the rules are that if you don't answer a question within 3 seconds, then you need to gulp down one tequila shot. We will ask each other a total of 5 questions and the questions can vary from person to person. Is everyone okay with it?'

'I don't drink like you all,' Sanaya responded.

'You don't have a choice, darling. All you can do is save yourself by giving answers within 3 seconds,' Yuvi laughed.

'Let's start with Vikrant. Sanaya you ask him the questions. That will make him more nervous,' Yuvi teased him.

'Ok cool. So Vikrant baby, here is your first question. What's the first thing you notice about the opposite sex?' Yuvi couldn't stop laughing at her question. Vikrant stared at him, trying to think and change his answer. Yuvi picked up two oranges from the table and held them out to Vikrant, much to his embarrassment. Yuvi told him his time was going to be up and he must hurry. Vikrant gave an angry look at Yuvi and turned towards Sanaya.

'Thighs. I love girls who have perfectly toned thighs,' he answered changing the answer at the last moment.

'Crap. You know you are lying. Who looks at girls' thighs?' Yuvi almost fell down laughing.

'You ass. I will take my revenge. I will ask you the same question in front of Kashish and then I will see what your answer is,' Vikrant said.

'Ok chill. Time for the next question. What's the worst thing you did as a kid?' Sanaya asked him. It was a fairly simple question this time.

'I stuck chewing gum in my teacher's hair, the same one I hated the most for giving me low marks in exams. I did it just to take revenge and then she suspended me,' Vikrant smiled.

Yuvi and Sanaya stared at him in shock. They couldn't believe Vikrant could do such things. Vikrant promised them not to talk about that episode any further and that he will tell them the entire story some other time.

'If you were to name one piece of clothing that describes you, the best what would it be?' asked Sanaya.

'Now that's not fair. What sort of question is this?' Vikrant said.

'Your three seconds are over and here is your shot,' said Yuvi handing him the glass.

Within no time, Vikrant gulped down the drink. He felt a bit tipsy as he was not used to drinking tequila but he had no other choice.

'Next one please,' he said trying to keep his eyes wide open.

'If you could have an unlimited storage of one thing, what would it be?' Sanaya asked with a smile on her face.

'I'd rather lose than answer that question. Give me the drink. I lose,' Vikrant said.

His answer was blue films but he couldn't have said that in front of Sanaya. The result of lying was that he had to gulp down two shots at a time for skipping the question on purpose.

'Here is your final question. Which act of your girlfriend drives you crazy?'

Vikrant could feel the lounge spinning rapidly around him. Everything seemed like a blur.

He thought for a while and answered, 'Our first kiss baby. It was so seductive. Your lips on mine and your tongue exploring mine. I want to kiss you right now. I love you so much.'

Sanaya told Vikrant to keep a check on control his desires as Yuvi was watching. Yuvi couldn't stop laughing looking at Vikrant. They were enjoying themselves to the fullest. Vikrant hugged Sanaya and told her how much he loved her. In the meanwhile, Yuvi had downed more than six shots of vodka. He doped at the same time. After Vikrant, it was Yuvi's ass on fire. He skipped the first couple of questions and had to gulp down 2 shots as punishment.

'Yuvi, you have got to answer the next question. What is your wildest fantasy?' Vikrant asked.

'Now that depends on who the girl is.'

'Bastard, I obviously mean with Kashish. Not with anyone else. Give me Kashish's number. Let me call her and tell her that Yuvi's wildest fantasy is not with her but with someone else.'

Vikrant was taking full advantage of teasing Yuvi.

'If you don't answer this question, you will lose,' said Sanaya pointing to the tequila shot.

'Ok, so here goes. My wildest fantasy is to make out on a beach during night when no one is watching,' Yuvi answered. His answer made no difference as he had already lost by then.

'Are you checking how much the bill is?' Vikrant asked Yuvi. They had ordered too many drinks.

'Chill dude. I have my Dad's credit card with me. Why worry?' Yuvi laughed.

'Yuvi, here's your final question. Which girl arouses you and makes you want to pounce on her that moment itself? It can be anyone—an actress or a model—but not your girlfriend.'

Yuvi thought for a while and answered, 'Anamika'!

His answer left everyone stunned. Did he have a burning desire for Anamika inside him which he had kept hidden for long? Was he infatuated with her? Did he take her name just for the game or did he really meant it? Vikrant and Sanaya didn't know how to react.

'Anamika… Anamika…Where is she? Sanaya go and call her. Why is she not with us? I think she overslept because of the headache,' Yuvi screamed.

He shut his eyes for a moment trying to figure out what he had just said. What was in her that awakened his fantasies? Or was it just after weed effect? He wanted to end it once and for all but didn't have any way to do it. He wanted to grab her and ask her an answer to all those questions but didn't have the courage to do so. He gulped another drink down.

Vikrant asked Sanaya to go and check on Anamika. Vikrant was surprised to see Yuvi in such a state. He had never behaved like that before and was used to smoking and taking drugs. Vikrant felt like he didn't know this new Yuvi since he was behaving like a completely different person. Vikrant splashed some water on his face to get him back to his senses while Sanaya left the lounge to check on Anamika.

'Ya Sanaya?' Vikrant asked her over the phone.

'Vikrant, Anamika is not opening the door and neither is she picking up my call,' Sanaya told him worriedly.

'She must have kept her phone on silent and gone off to sleep. Tell the receptionist to give you a duplicate key to the room. If you still can't find her in the room, look for her near the pool side. She might have gone out for a stroll all by herself. Come soon. We are waiting,' Vikrant instructed her and kept the phone down.

Sanaya did as was told. She went to the reception and told them the entire story. They handed her the duplicate key and asked her to alert them if something was wrong. Sanaya prayed it wouldn't have to come to that. But as she climbed up the stairs, she sensed something was wrong. As it was night-time, the passage leading to the room was deserted and even the slightest sound was enough to make her jump out of her skin. She inserted the key in the keyhole and looked sideways to see if she could spot anyone. There was not a person in sight. She opened the door and to her dismay she found no one inside. The room looked untouched. The bed was neatly made up and the dress Anamika had decided to wear to the party was hanging in the cupboard. Anamika's absence worried her. She went to the pool side hoping to find her there, but that area was deserted too. No one swam at this time of the night. With every passing minute, her worries increased. She had absolutely no clue about Anamika's whereabouts. She ran to the lounge to inform Vikrant and Yuvi that Anamika was missing.

'How's that possible? Where can she go? She is not a child that she can get lost,' Vikrant said trying to pacify the other two.

'She must be with Anurag,' Yuvi stated in a matter-of-fact tone.

'Anurag? Are you in your senses? What are you talking about?' Sanaya was surprised at Yuvi's answer.

'Yes, I know what I'm saying. She must be with Anurag,' Yuvi repeated again.

Sanaya was on the verge of losing her temper but Vikrant calmed her down by holding her by her waist.

'How do you know? How can Anurag come all the way to Daman? He is in Delhi,' Vikrant explained.

'Yes dude, but he had messaged me that he was not going to leave her and me for how we had insulted him. Through his friends he came to know that we are here. I got a message from him saying he will kill us in Daman itself,' Yuvi answered.

This was another shock for Vikrant and Sanaya. They were already worried about Anamika's sudden disappearance and now this. They panicked, as they didn't know what to do next.

'See, we have no choice but to search for her. We don't know anyone here and we can't get the local police involved as it will create unnecessary troubles. They might alert our parents. Sanaya, you stay here near the gate and check the resort premises while Yuvi and I will look for her on the beach. She might have gone for a late night walk. Don't get scared and keep calling her continuously. She might pick up the phone,' Vikrant instructed.

Vikrant couldn't believe what was happening. All he could do was wish that Anamika was safe and sound. It was his plan to get everybody to Daman and try and reunite the band. He had forced both of them to come along and now this incident had occurred. Never in his wildest dreams had he thought that his decision would turn into a nightmare. Not showing how panicked he was, he regained his composure and began with the search mission. While Vikrant decided to look for her at Devka beach, Yuvi took Jampore beach so that they could cover two places at the same time.

'Anamika… Anamika… Please come back. Where are you? Can you hear me?' Vikrant screamed but did not get a response. He was sad, depressed, and low on confidence. He returned back to the resort hoping to find Anamika already there. He tried calling her but now her phone was unreachable. Yuvi was yet to return from Jampore beach.

Vikrant kept shouting her name at the resort as loud as he could but all he could hear was his own echo. The other guests at the hotel came to him and asked him what was wrong. He showed them a picture of Anamika and told them how she had gone missing. The guests promised to alert him if they saw her in the hotel premises. Just when Vikrant was about to call the police, he saw Yuvi approaching.

'Did you see her anywhere or did she pick up your call?' Vikrant asked Yuvi with a worried face.

Yuvi remained silent and didn't utter a word. He was looking down and avoiding direct eye contact with Vikrant which Vikrant found odd. Maybe he was doped out completely and had no clue where he was.

'Speak up. What's wrong with you? Did you see Anamika at the beach?' Vikrant screamed trying to shake Yuvi from trance.

'Vikrant, leave him alone. I don't think he is in a state to talk. He looks completely doped out. Let him go to his room and sleep. In this state, he will not be of much help in the search anyway. Before he falls down here and creates a scene, take him to his room and put him to sleep,' Sanaya suggested.

Vikrant took Yuvi to his room. He kept wondering where Anamika was. How could she go away without even informing anyone? Vikrant double-checked her room but everything was in place. She had not even taken anything with her. Not even her camera. He shuddered to think Anurag was involved in her disappearance.

Sanaya came to the room and said, 'I think we should inform the police before it gets worse. We have looked for her wherever we could. There is no point in waiting till morning. If whatever Yuvi said is true, we should inform the police.'

Vikrant took all the blame on him. He should never have planned this trip nor should he have taken a step to bring everyone together. He sat on the couch weeping in Sanaya's arms. He couldn't find a way out and the night terrified him more.

Sometimes silence cuts deeper than a knife. Sanaya and Vikrant's silence was getting to them. They had no clue whether to wait for Yuvi to regain normalcy state or walk to the nearby police station to file a missing complaint. Vikrant thought he shouldn't have convinced Anamika to come along. What hurts worst? Saying something and wishing you hadn't? Or not saying something and wishing you had?

'I am uniquely different and I love to win.' 'Vikrant darling, don't worry as I am always with you. If you don't get your metro girl then we will be together.' 'Bhaiya or Bhabi ko badhai ho badhai.' Anamika's words kept ringing in his ears. He looked at Sanaya who was fighting the tears in her eyes. They hoped and prayed everything would be fine by morning. Why is

it that when things are going perfect for you, all of a sudden a million things go wrong and flood away the good? Life isn't fair sometimes!

❧

Mia Bella
15th September, 2013, Around 7 am

One of the hardest decisions you'll ever make in life is choosing whether to walk away or stay back and keep trying harder. We sometimes take decisions and make promises and they go on to haunt us later on in life. One should not take any decisions when one is angry and should not make any promises when one is happy. Vikrant had done both. He had taken the decision of going on a trip when nothing seemed to work his way and had promised himself that he would bring back VAYU, but the night changed everything.

I never knew life could be so unpredictable. So much so that within seconds you are lifted from heaven and put in hell to burn. I kept on thinking about Anurag and how the feeling of anger and revenge can actually devastate a person's life. I was able to feel what Vikrant, Yuvi, and Sanaya might have gone through in those few hours of panic where they could see no way ahead of them. I could feel their pain. A happy-go-lucky girl who was adored by her friends vanishes in thin air with not a trace left behind. Even the mere thought gave me goosebumps. What might have happened to her? Did Anurag kill her? How brutal could a person get?

I couldn't control myself and asked Vikrant, 'Where did she go? Did you find her later?'

Vikrant took a deep breath and said, 'Yes, we did.'

'Where?' Sakshi asked.

'I was so upset and was just crying in Sanaya's arms. My brain was blocked and I couldn't think of anything that moment. Yuvi was drunk and not at all in a state to give any suggestions. I was alone and this terrified me more. I couldn't send Sanaya anywhere fearing if Anurag found her, he might take her away too. Sanaya suggested I file a police complaint but I was afraid as I did not want us to land in trouble unnecessarily, especially because we had lied at home to come to Daman,' Vikrant explained.

'So did you file a police complaint?' I asked.

I was curious to know what had happened to her. I kept my fingers crossed hoping she returned safely to the resort.

'Yes, we did. I had no choice but to follow Sanaya's suggestion as we had no clue where she had gone. With a heavy heart, I went to the nearest police station and told them everything. After a routine inquiry, they took her photograph and jotted down a few details which would help in her identification. They asked us so many questions and almost hinted at the fact that we were responsible for her disappearance. We were not even allowed to leave Daman as the cops doubted us too. We were helpless because we were in an alien land. They told us that they will inform us as soon as they have something concrete to tell. They told us to inform our parents till morning ourselves or they would do it for us.'

Vikrant put up a brave front but I knew the amount of pain he must have carried inside his heart. If just listening to their story was making me so anxious, I could imagine what they might have gone through. Sometimes it's difficult to decide what's wrong or right. A lie that brings a smile on your face or a truth that brings tears in your eyes. Vikrant and Sanaya had lied to themselves that Anamika would return safely but the truth was that she had gone missing for whole night and the possibility of finding her seemed very bleak.

'Then what happened? Did the cops find her?' Sakshi questioned again biting her nails.

Vikrant nodded and said, 'The Daman police found a girl in the morning in an unconscious state. They did not give any details on the phone but told us to come to the police station within an hour to identify if it was her. We ran to the police station from where the cops took us to hospital. There she was! Our Anamika lying in a bruised state on the hospital bed! We didn't know how to react when we saw her—whether to be happy that we had found her or sad that we had found her in this condition. We could see that she had grave physical injuries on her body.'

'Who was behind her condition? How did it happen and how did police find her?' I asked.

The girl who always seemed to smile, cried; who was always held together, had fallen apart; who lifted everyone else up, needed someone to hold her up. People come into your life for a reason; they shape you, they form you, they may even break you. Was Anamika's meeting with Anurag a mistake? When Vikrant told us who was behind it, we were shocked!

Sometimes what you expect from a friend, you get from a stranger, and sometimes what you expect from a stranger, you get from a friend!

Is Friendship a Product?

4th October, 2012

Someone once said that death is not the greatest loss in life. The greatest loss is what dies inside us while we're alive. No matter how hard Vikrant tried, he could sense he was moving towards a slow and painful death. Death of their friendship, their love, and their bonding! How strange it was that the day he managed to bring VAYU together, he lost Anamika! The day he managed to propose to Sanaya, he lost happiness! It was their first night together and they couldn't even smile. Anamika was not his childhood friend but the bonding that they had developed in the past few months was something special. She treated him like a brother and her absence was killing Vikrant every minute. Yuvi did not seem very bothered about Anamika's disappearance as he was never close to her anyway. He wanted to win her over and show his dominance over her but that night he was hardly in his senses to even bother. After coming back from the police station, they just sat quietly in their room waiting to hear a knock on the door by Anamika. But no one knocked till morning. Life without friends is like the world without colour and Vikrant could feel it that night.

'Hi guys. Good morning,' Yuvi said as he entered Vikrant's room the next morning. Sanaya was asleep as she had been up all night cradling Vikrant in her arms.

'Yuvi, thank God you're up. What had happened to you yesterday, yaar? I have never seen you getting so tipsy ever. Please tell me if you saw her at Jampore beach. You didn't answer yesterday and went straight to your room before we could talk any further,' Vikrant said in a nervous tone.

'Nothing,' Yuvi replied in one word.

He seemed upset. Something was killing him from inside. He didn't answer any of Vikrant questions which made Vikrant furious. He could sense there was something worse coming their way. He promised that he wasn't going to let Anurag live happily if he had done anything to Anamika. Vikrant tried every possible way to provoke Yuvi to speak up but Yuvi kept mum. Do you ever feel the need for someone's arms around you in your most trying times? Yuvi was feeling the same! When Vikrant and Sanaya told him they had filed a missing complaint report at the nearby police station, Yuvi's face turned blue. He was shivering badly. Vikrant could tell something was going on in his mind. He wanted to confess something but wasn't finding the courage to do so.

'Why did you do that? That was not needed, right? We should have…' Yuvi couldn't complete his sentence.

Before Vikrant could explain why he had taken that step, he got a call from the same police station that they had found an unconscious girl on the beach and had admitted her to the nearby hospital.

'Which hospital, inspector? Okay… We will be there in few minutes,' Vikrant stammered and continued, 'Okay thank you. We will be there.'

Yuvi was looking at him anxiously and by now, even Sanaya had got up hearing the loud ringtone.

'What happened?' she asked.

'They have called us to Anand hospital which is located near Jampore beach. We should leave right now,' Vikrant said as he got up to get ready.

All the way to the hospital, no one spoke. They had sensed that they had landed in deep trouble with no way out. Was she alive? What was she doing at Jampore beach in the middle of the night? Did Anurag call her there? If then, did he hit her and left her to die on the beach? Why hadn't Yuvi been able to find her when he had gone looking for her at the beach? And why hadn't she attempted to call anyone of them? Only Anamika had the answer to their questions. As soon as they got down from the taxi, they rushed to the ICU ward.

'You can't meet her unless we have done our routine inquiry,' a senior inspector ordered us as we tried to get in.

'But what happened to her and why is she here?' Vikrant and Sanaya spoke together.

'Is she alright?' Yuvi asked in a low tone as if he was guilty.

'Not really. We just had a word with the doctors and according to them, she has physical injuries on her body and is not in a stable state. She was brought here in an unconscious state and hence we have to wait for her to wake up as only she can tell us what exactly had happened,' the senior inspector answered.

'What do you mean by physical injuries? What do the reports say?' Sanaya stammered.

'It means someone tried to get physical with her without her consent. Now whether the intention was to kill her or rape her, we don't know yet. But yes, he definitely tried to get physical with her. We think she was alone on the beach when this incident occurred. We got a call from a few fishermen early in the morning saying they had found a girl lying unconscious on the beach. When we reached the shore, she was not only unconscious but was also bleeding badly.'

The inspector peeped in through the glass door to see if there was any improvement in Anamika's condition. Vikrant was heartbroken listening to all this and couldn't hold back his tears. Sanaya tried to console him but it was of no use. Yuvi stood there with an expressionless face. Vikrant wanted to tell the cops about Anurag and the message that he had sent but preferred to keep silent and wait for Anamika to regain consciousness. All three of them went into the waiting room as they were not allowed to meet before the police inquiry.

Vikrant was extremely upset with the incident. A girl who was someone's child, a girl who was someone's sister, a girl

174

who was someone in her own eyes had now been injured beyond repair. Only Yuvi knew what had happened last night. He wanted to tell them everything but feared losing them. Somehow he gathered courage and with a stammering voice he told Vikrant and Sanaya that he wanted to confess everything. Vikrant and Sanaya looked at each other with a quizzical expression. Everybody says love hurts but that's not true. Loneliness hurts. Rejection hurts. Loss hurts. Love is the one thing that makes everything better again and Yuvi hoped they still loved him even after what he was about to tell them.

'Vikrant, I know you won't believe what I am going to confess right now but it's true. Please don't misunderstand me. I know I have done a mistake and I am guilty as charged. I am even ready to suffer for my mistake as I know it's unforgivable. Maybe I will lose you all and will have to spend my entire life alone but I can't live with this guilt. I thought I will not tell this to anyone as no one will come to know about it, but seeing Anamika here like this has shattered me. It's all because of me. Things could have been different last night but I screwed it all up and I still don't know why. I kept asking myself that why did I take that step but I had no answer and I still don't have an answer now. I know you won't accept it easily but that's the sad truth. If Anamika is lying here today in this condition, then it's all because of me. Only I am responsible for it and no one else. I don't know what happened to me but… It's not that it happened all of a sudden. Remember I had told you…'

Vikrant interrupted Yuvi, 'Yuvi what's wrong? Calm yourself down first. What is your point exactly? We all are responsible for today's scenario. You can speak your heart out.'

Yuvi continued, 'Everybody goes through some things in life that changes them in a way that they can never go back to being the person they were before. Last night changed me in a similar way. Now I cannot go back to being the person I once was. As I told you, it was not all of a sudden. Remember, I had told you that there is that oomph factor in Anamika which attracted me to her even though I hated her carefree attitude to the core? When I met her for the first time in our college auditorium, I felt like she had that wow factor in her which impressed me a great deal. Though I was committed to Kashish, I couldn't help myself from staring at her sexy figure and that's human tendency. Men are made like that. I thought that she was flirting with me because she would try and come close to me. Maybe I misunderstood her actions—I do not know. Her relationship with Anurag made me feel like she was a girl who you could take to parties just to show her off to your friends. It was completely my perception and it was developed on the basis of her casual attitude towards late night parties and drinks. I never knew her before so I was not aware of how she was as a person. When I got acquainted with her, I realized that though she exposed a bit much, she was a nice person at heart. Remember Vikrant, you were against her relationship? You asked me how she could agree to Anurag's proposal just to overcome her fear. I was the one who convinced you that she was not wrong and that her situation had made her take that decision. Day by day, my infatuations increased and I even tried to talk to her about it but I never got a chance. Once I tried telling her in the car on our way to some place, but since Anurag had come along, I couldn't find the right opportunity. Plus, I thought of Kashish and our four-year-old relationship, and how much she had supported me. I couldn't do this to her. Do you ever regret making a decision? I regret the day I decided to give her equal space in our band though she never was an active participant and just wanted to enjoy outings and parties. Her dream was to be a part of one of the best bands in town but my dream was to make our band the best in town. Soon she started getting more popular than me and that made me jealous. It was our band and we had put equal efforts, so why was she getting the maximum publicity? I couldn't digest it and each day it killed me from inside. I wanted to harm the same skin she showed off to win fans. Though I hated her more each day, I was also in a way attracted to her. Probably because she was a complete contrast to Kashish. I controlled my emotions for the sake of the band. But when her relationship screwed everything we had earned with so much of hard work, I lost it. I had warned her so many times to keep her personal relationship away from the band but she didn't listen.

'When you told me about this trip, I thought I will refuse to avoid facing Anamika since I knew it could lead to something unwanted. For your friendship, I agreed to come for this trip. Kashish explained to me that Anamika was not wrong on her part and that she was like this by nature. While you and Sanaya were spending time together, Anamika came to me and apologized for whatever had happened. However, it only takes one second to break someone's trust but it takes an entire lifetime to rebuild it. I didn't want to create a scene as I knew how important this trip was for your relationship and I accepted her apology. But there comes a time in life when we realize that we cannot force love, respect, or friendship. If it's not from the heart, then it's false and meaningless!!

'I had realized that our relationship could never be the same again. But strange are our emotions. Even when you know that things won't go your way, you still take a chance. That evening when you proposed to Sanaya, we both were equally happy and casually hugged each other. The hug changed something in me. I wanted to feel her. I wanted to see how wild she could get. I wanted to see if she could satisfy my urge. But fate had a different plan in mind. Yesterday when I was alone before the party, I thought of going to the beach just to chill out by myself for a bit. But I had no idea that it was high tide until I had gone too deep into the water. The waves almost engulfed me. I screamed for help, as I was not a good swimmer. I was lucky that the security guard heard my screams in time and came running to save me. I didn't tell you about this episode as I wasn't hurt and I did not want to spoil your first evening together as a couple. In those few seconds, I wanted to live my life just as I wished. The fear of facing death changed me completely. Now I wanted to fulfil all my fantasies because facing death had made me realize that we never know what will happen the next moment. Later that night when we went to look for Anamika I was not at all in my senses.

'We should never start a task if we don't intend to finish it and we should never speak up if we don't mean it. When I saw Anamika alone yesterday on the beach I decided to strike a conversation with her and break the barriers that lied between us. I spoke things I never meant. I don't even remember everything but I will try...'

Jampore Beach, Daman

'Anamika what are you doing here?' Yuvi asked her when he saw her sitting alone on the sea shore.

'I just want to spend some time alone,' Anamika answered.

'Are you alright?'

Yuvi came and sat next to her. She was surprised by the amount of concern he was showing.

'Yes. I am so confused about where my life is going. I still wonder if I'm capable of loving anyone. Anyway, what's wrong with you? You look drunk,' Anamika added.

She wanted to spend time alone away from everyone to think about her future and her life, so she had kept her phone on silent mode. She was in no mood to take calls from anyone. She also wanted to avoid Yuvi's party because she sensed Yuvi was not very keen in spending time with her. She didn't want to spoil Vikrant and Sanaya's night and thus preferred to spend some time alone by herself on the beach.

'There is something about you which attracts me to you. You are one of those girls who look nice when they are drunk. I wanted to express my feelings since a long time but I never got a chance,' Yuvi exclaimed.

Anamika was feeling odd at the sudden change in his behaviour. She knew very well that Yuvi loved Kashish from the core of his heart. She told him to watch what he was saying as he was drunk. She further added that whatever he was up to was wrong. But Yuvi was in no mood to listen to her. He tried to catch hold of her forcefully. He held her by her waist and planted a kiss on her mouth. Anamika tried to push him away but he was too big for her to handle.

'This body makes me crazy. I want to ram you right here on the beach. I want to see my fantasy turn into a reality. Oh bitch! Let me taste you tonight. Let me feel your body.'

Yuvi forcefully pushed her to the ground and jumped on top of her. She tried to resist with all her might but he was too strong for her. He tried to kiss her neck and her mouth. She tried to scream but he shut her mouth by placing his hand on top of it. After some time, she surrendered to his wishes. She lied there like a dead body while Yuvi devoured her as if she was a piece of meat. Tears trickled down her face. Anamika felt like she was losing a friend forever. The feeling was worse. The more Yuvi tried to force himself physically on her, the farther he went mentally. By the time he went up and left, she had turned inanimate.

Anand Hospital, Daman

'Excuse me. The doctors have given their final report to us. They said that she was physically assaulted. You need to treat her with love and pamper her without giving her stress. Anamika is being kept under observation for 24 hours. We are leaving for the day but if needed, we will come back. Do you have any clue what was she was doing so late at the beach?' the senior inspector inquired.

A wave of silence filled the air. They knew what had happened last night but couldn't say anything in front of the cops. They simply shook their heads to say 'no'. A lost or a broken friendship hurts, but what hurts more is the realization that they weren't a true friend to begin with.

What Was Her Fault?

Jampore Beach

Mistakes make you realize that sometimes there are no time outs and no second chances. Anamika couldn't go back and change what had happened during the music festival but she had tried to break the wall of grudges between Yuvi and her. It was Yuvi who had broken all the trust. But what hurt her the most was that the pain was inflicted by none other than Yuvi whom she had regarded as a friend. He should have either forgiven her or taken her out of his future altogether. Why are some friends only there when you are a convenience to them. Yuvi had the same attitude towards her and she couldn't do anything to change it. When Yuvi told them about the party he was hosting for Vikrant and Sanaya at the resort, Anamika felt Yuvi was not looking forward to her coming, so she chose to avoid the party by staying alone. She told Yuvi that she had bad headache and stayed back in the room. But she wanted to spend some time with herself to introspect, so she decided to go to Jampore beach without informing anyone. She wanted to peacefully think about her relationships, friendship, love, and the future.

She sat alone thinking about the incident that had changed their lives forever.

If it was my fault, then let me walk away from you all. Anurag did those things on purpose because he was serious about our relationship whereas all I wanted was to get over my fear. I had never crossed my limits. I never slept with him. If just roaming with him makes me a slut, then it was my fault. If spending time with him makes me a slut, then it was my fault. I never thought things would turn so ugly. My only mistake was that I kept him in the dark about my real intentions. However, looking at the image he had created for himself in the past, I never thought Anurag would get serious about me and would hurt our entire group. He tried to approach me so many times but I never talked to him after that incident. He should not have hurt you all and that was his fault. What more could I have done apart from ignoring him completely even after knowing he was a changed man and wanted me in his life anyhow? What more could have I done to prove my loyalty towards the band and our friendship?

Anamika was recounting her past when Yuvi came and sat beside her, inquiring about why she was on the beach alone at that time.

Yuvi tried to flirt with her which made her feel awkward as she knew that Yuvi loved Kashish dearly. She felt his sudden change in behaviour was because he was heavily under the influence of alcohol and drugs. Yuvi forced himself on her even though she resisted.

'Yuvi, what are you doing. Please leave. This is wrong. Leave right now or else I will scream. You are drunk and not in your senses.' Though she kept screaming for help, Yuvi didn't show any mercy on her. The area was so isolated that no one could hear her scream.

'I need you right now. I want to calm myself and make you my slave, you slut. If you can sleep with that Anurag, then why not with me? I just love your curves. I want to go deep inside you, my slave,' Yuvi hissed as the feeling of revenge engulfed him.

He had lost it completely by then. Yuvi not just tore her clothes that night, he tore her heart apart. He used her body to fulfill his sexual fantasy, ignoring the soul that resided within her. Each time he hit her, she screamed louder. She struggled to release herself from his forceful grip. Yuvi came real close to her and whispered 'Bitch I wish you weren't alive'. She thought the same. She did not want to survive. He hardened his grip on her hands and covered her mouth. She finally gave up and closed her eyes wishing the time to pass by quickly so that the next time she opened her eyes, he wouldn't be standing there. He pushed himself inside her harder and harder and she felt unbearable pain. She couldn't believe it was happening to her. She stopped screaming after some time as she realized the torture was over. But the pain was going to last forever. After a few minutes, Yuvi left her alone to die. She lay there with torn clothes, nail scratches on her body, and blood all around. The ones you trust the most are the ones who shouldn't be trusted. With each lie, the nature of the relationship changes. But what happened last night was not a lie. Yet the relationship had changed. Sometimes the greatest lessons learned are taught by those whom you label as your 'friends'.

❦

Anand Hospital, Daman
4th October, 2012

She survived but had no hope left from her life. She felt it would have been better had she died that day. At least she wouldn't have to live the nightmare her life had become now. She had managed to overcome her phobia of ragging, but how could she overcome this nightmare?

She opened her eyes and saw everyone standing in front of her. She tried to smile looking at Vikrant and Sanaya. She had high fever and her body shivered. When she saw Yuvi standing behind them, she immediately looked the other way in disgust.

'What happened last night?' the senior inspector asked.

'Nothing inspector. All I can remember is that I was drunk and that someone held me from behind and tried to force himself on me. After that I do not remember anything,' whispered Anamika in a low voice.

Her answer shocked not just Yuvi but everyone standing there who knew Yuvi was behind the incident. No one had any clue what Anamika was upto and why she had tried to save Yuvi even though he had assaulted her so badly. Before the cops could ask her any more questions, the doctors arrived on the scene and told them to leave so she could rest. They suggested shifting her to a rehabilitation centre for her quick recovery once she was back in Delhi as she had lost her emotional balance. Vikrant thanked the doctors for their help and shut the door to Anamika's room.

Everyone was in a state of shock and Vikrant was completely heartbroken. He wanted to bring back VAYU and what had happened instead! What hurt him more was that he had lost both his friends. The ones on whom he had relied upon.

Yuvi's guilt was destroying him every minute and he didn't talk with anyone after returning to the resort. Anamika's face haunted him in his dreams whenever he tried to sleep. When Kashish came to know about it, she was furious, dejected, and heartbroken. She sent Yuvi a message:

'I thought our relationship would last forever. But now it's time to walk away. You lied, cheated, and broke all the promises.

I deserve better than that. What was my fault? One day you're going to wake up and realize how much I loved you, but I will not be by your side. One day you'll realize how much I've done for you and how much you have taken me for granted. I am leaving you, not because I have stopped loving you but because I don't want a husband like you, a father like you under whose arms a girl can't be safe. Sorry, you're not my type. Bye forever Yuvi. I wish you good luck.'

Sitting in the police station, he re-read the message Kashish had sent him last night. He didn't have the strength to look into her eyes and for that matter, even Vikrant and Sanaya. The moment he confessed his crime to the cops, he was handcuffed and put behind bars. Anamika lost her self-confidence that night but Yuvi lost his life. But Yuvi still couldn't figure out why Anamika had lied to the cops and not taken his name. He could have lied to everyone but his soul arrested him. Love is just a word, till you show it. Guilt and sin are just words, till you commit it. Yuvi could have saved himself but his guilt had arrested him.

It was ironical that Vikrant and Sanaya would never be able to celebrate the day their relationship had kicked off. VAYU was just a thing of the past now. The A of the VAYU was struggling to survive while the Y of VAYU was struggling to understand why he had committed the crime. Sometimes you have to take a step back and realize what's important in your life, what you can live with, but more importantly what you can't live without.

Love isn't easy. There will be hard times, there will be great times. The key to a successful relationship is to find your way through the hard times and cherish the great times. Vikrant and Sanaya had faced a hard time from the beginning of their relationship but they were finally going to have a good time now. Forgive and forget seems good in some cases but in Vikrant and Sanaya's case, moving on seemed appropriate.

The next day, Anamika was brought to Delhi and was shifted to a rehabilitation centre nearby. She had lost her confidence and needed a strong support system. Her family, Vikrant, and Sanaya stood by her side and gave her all the help and support she needed. Yuvi had taken her outspoken and free-minded nature for granted and abused her. Now, even the touch of her father or her doctor sent her screaming. Days passed by but her condition didn't improve. In the meantime, Anurag had come to know about the entire episode. He started paying regular visits to the rehab centre. Everyone could see that he was not the same person anymore and that he truly loved Anamika. But every night she screamed in pain as she recounted the dreadful night. She wanted the world to see and understand her pain. She wanted to be held tight, so tight that her fears fade away. She wanted to be kissed by someone who loved her and who could wipe all her tears away. She wanted to be told that she is not a disappointment and she doesn't bring shame anymore.

When a leaf falls from a tree who should be blamed? The wind that blows it away? The tree that lets it fall? Or the leaf itself that grows tired of holding on?

Mia Bella
15th September, 2013, Around 8 am

Sitting in Mia Bella and listening to the journey of VAYU—the band had transported me to another world altogether. Anamika—a girl who had stood behind Vikrant as a true friend, a girl who had made VAYU popular, a girl who could never gain Yuvi's confidence and yet tried to be his good friend, a girl who always made everyone smile and overcome her fears—had to go through so much in life. Even after a year, Vikrant had tears in his eyes while narrating the incident. When Vikrant told me that Anurag was paying regular visits to the rehab centre, it kind of surprised me.

'Vikrant, what brought the sudden change in Anurag? How did he start taking care of Anamika?' I asked.

'I mean it,' replied Vikrant.

'But how did it happen?' I asked curiously.

'We had misunderstood him completely. Anamika was having a casual affair with Anurag but he wasn't. He was truly in love with her. The night when he tried to get close with Anamika, it was because he felt their relationship had reached that level. And when she told him to stop, he did. Later when Anamika broke up with him, he followed her everywhere and tried to make her understand that he was a changed person but she didn't give a damn. He wanted to tell her that he really loved her and wanted to be with her for a lifetime. However, when he came to know what had happened with Anamika in Daman, he came running to the rehab centre and convinced all of us that he was a changed man. As the days passed by, he stood by her like a strong pillar and to an extent it helped in her recovery.'

Anamika deserved love and attention. She deserved every pampering in the world and getting it from Anurag brought a big smile on my face. How many chances do you give someone to prove they are not what you thought they were all along? Everyone in life is going to hurt you but you just have to figure out which people are worth the pain. On the one hand, Anamika had given Yuvi many chances but he still stabbed her in the back. On the other hand was Anurag who seized the one opportunity she gave him to prove that he really loved her.

'What about Kashish? Is she still in touch with you?'

'Never. Neither I tried calling her nor did she. She used to be with us only because of Yuvi and when the reason itself vanished, there was no point in us keeping touch,' Vikrant stated.

'But why didn't Anamika take Yuvi's name in front of the police, especially when everyone knew that it was Yuvi who had assaulted her?' Sakshi asked.

Vikrant said, 'I remember asking her the same question once she had started responding to treatment and could speak a little.'

'Then what did she say?' I asked.

'That she loved him.'

I couldn't believe my ears. Anamika loved Yuvi! Now I realized why she had remained silent and suffered all the pain alone, why she had chosen to face the brutal world by herself without even uttering a word. If Yuvi hadn't surrendered to the cops on his own will, no one would have known anything about it. That's the reason she gave him so many chances despite his odd behaviour. To love somebody isn't just a strong feeling; it's a decision, a judgement, and a promise. Unknowingly, Yuvi had broken them all. Yuvi was certainly not made for her. Every girl deserves a guy who can make her forget her heart was ever broken.

Rehab Centre, Delhi
10th June, 2013

'How are you feeling now?' Vikrant inquired. He had come to visit Anamika in the rehab centre along with Sanaya.

'I am fine now. All the credit goes to my family who've supported me, to you guys who gave ,me a helping hand, and to Anurag who helped me recover even when I was afraid to even take a step ahead,' Anamika answered.

'We are glad to know that you've realized who your true well-wishers are. That's why people say we should take chances in life. If you wouldn't have taken a chance and accepted Anurag's proposal, you wouldn't have recovered with such speed,' Vikrant said and looking at Anurag he continued, 'Anurag buddy, we are sorry that we misunderstood you. We never thought you loved her for real. We are glad that you are with Anamika. Thank you so much for taking care of my little baby sister.'

'Vikrant, I never knew the true meaning of love until I met Anamika. Taking care of her makes me happy and that's my responsibility towards my love. I never got a chance to say sorry to you, Sanaya, but today I apologize. I hope you forgive me.'

'Anurag, I've forgiven you long back and if you wouldn't have broken up with me, I wouldn't have met Vikrant ever. I should be eternally grateful to you,' Sanaya said holding Vikrant's hand firmly.

Anurag helped Anamika to sit on the bed and helped her drink coffee. Sometimes a cup of coffee and a good friend can make your life much better.

'Anamika, can I ask you one thing?'said Vikrant.

Anamika nodded taking a sip of the coffee with Anurag's help.

'In the hospital when that inspector asked you about the incident, why did you lie to them? All of us knew Yuvi was behind it, so why did you lie to the cops?' Vikrant inquired. He wanted to clear his doubts.

Anamika remained silent for a few seconds and then glanced at Anurag. Vikrant could see a tear drop rolling down her cheeks which Anurag wiped off with his hand.

She looked at Vikrant and said, 'Because I loved him. I never told him about it as he was in a serious relationship with Kashish. Heck, he didn't even see me as a friend, so how could I have told him? When he forced me to get intimate with him that night, I tried to stop him as it was wrong. I meant nothing to him and neither did he know that I loved him. In those 30 minutes, he treated me as a toy on which you lay your hands whenever you want and then throw away as per your wish. What hurt me the most was that the attacker was not a stranger but a guy whom I loved. I realized he was not my type.'

Anurag kept a finger on her lips telling her not to go into the details. She was barely recovering and he didn't want her to think about all of it again. Vikrant and Sanaya too changed the topic and moved to a discussion about music and upcoming bands.

If Anamika would have chosen to give up, she would have killed so many people around her who truly loved her and wanted her to do well in life. She had decided to be the author of her own destiny and not the victim of her circumstances. She had decided to live for those who wanted her to fight against all the odds. She had made sure that even the saddest of stories can have happy endings...!

Epilogue

Making millions of friends is not an achievement; a real achievement is making one friend who stands by you through thick and thin! Anamika had such friends in her life. They had stood by her like a family during her darkest days. While man has invented so many amazing things to cure diseases and illnesses, no one has been able to find the cure for the mental pain and trauma given by someone. Only time can heal such wounds! Anamika had fought with death and she now had reason to live. I was anxious to meet Anamika and before leaving Mia Bella early that morning, I managed to convince Vikrant to schedule a short visit to the rehab centre. After a bit of convincing, he agreed to take me along with him after lunch. The night had been memorable and worth every penny, but now I was curious to meet Anamika. Anuj, the manager of Mia Bella was equally supportive as he had allowed us to sit there till the wee hours of the morning. Sakshi and I hardly talked on our way back home as we were still zapped after listening to VAYU's story. We had become so engrossed in the story that we felt like we were a part of their lives. In the past few hours, we had lived and felt every small moment they had gone through. I dropped her by cab and then returned to my hotel room.

Being single doesn't always mean you're lonely and being in a relationship doesn't always mean you're happy. Was Yuvi lonely even after being in a relationship or was it just lust and jealousy that took over him that night. It was still a mystery to everyone after one year. Never take anyone or anything for granted because it only takes a second for a life to be altered forever. Yuvi was arrested by the cops after he had confessed to the crime. He had lost everything in his life. Fame, love, dignity, and even his friends. Yuvi had met two girls, Anamika and Kashish, and he had managed to betray both! Not just that, he had managed to betray even his band VAYU!

Kashish never contacted Vikrant and group after they all returned to Delhi from Daman and no one knew where she was. But Vikrant was sure she had moved on. She was not the sorts who would cry over a pathetic guy like Yuvi after knowing all that he had done. Why should we try holding onto the past when the future can be so much better. She was indeed a darling and deserved a person who treated her like an angel.

Vikrant and Sanaya had managed to hold on to their relationship and if Vikrant could change time, he'd go back to the moment they had met for the first time. Not to change anything but to experience it all over again. Even today when they travelled by the Metro, they remembered all the moments of the past. The best love story is not of Romeo and Juliet who died young but of our Grandpa and Grandma who grew old together. Similarly, Vikrant and Sanaya wouldn't let the day end without telling one another how much they meant to each other and the only argument they got into was who loved the other more. Well, they both loved each other equally!

Almost a year had passed since the incident and Anamika was trying to start afresh at the rehab centre. With Anurag's help, she was making a speedy recovery. Around him, she was happier than ever before. You don't realize how strong a person really is until you see them fight their weakest moment. Anamika had kicked the doors of sorrow to rebuild her life. In the beginning even the slight touch of a man would make her scream. But Anurag helped her overcome her trauma by being patient with her and pampering her like a baby. For once, someone actually wanted to be with her for a lifetime. As time passed, Anurag made her believe in love once again. Just when she thought everything was going wrong, Anurag had brought back that lovely smile on her face. Sometimes all the doors may be closed, but they aren't always locked.

Rehab Centre, Delhi
15th September, 2013

She lived! She learned! She loved! She helped! She got hurt! She feared! But today she smiled…When your passion and purpose is greater than your fears, you find a way to overcome them. She had found her way, she had found her love, she had found her friends, and today she smiled because she had fought depression, pain, and death! When I saw her from a distance, she was sitting with Anurag who was feeding her food. She was the exact replica of how Vikrant had described her. Her tattoo was visible from a distance and I felt glad to see her smiling once again. As she saw Vikrant and me walking towards her, she waved her hand at us, with a broad smile.

'Anamika, how are you?' Vikrant asked.

'I am fine now. Let's see when doctors allow me to go home. Maybe a month or so. But how come you are here today?' Anamika asked.

'Actually my friend wanted to meet you. This is Aditya from Mumbai. He was here for some official work and thought of meeting you.'

'Vikrant, you've started making friends online or what? As far as I know, you don't have any friends in Mumbai. Not any girlfriends, at least,' she smiled.

'Anurag tell her yaar. One day I will land in trouble because of her silly jokes. What will people think?' Vikrant said teasingly.

'By the way, why is he here to meet me? Neither am I a model, nor an actress. Now I'm not even a part of VAYU,' Anamika added.

'Can I tell you why?' I asked seeking permission from her to answer her question. She nodded and I continued, 'Though you are not a movie star or a model, you are still an inspiration. When Vikrant told me about your life's journey, I was amazed and was curious to meet the girl who had fought all the odds and had come out victorious. I was really inspired by you. You are so unique and Anurag you are a gem of a person. It's not easy to accept a girl after knowing so much but you did. Seriously, hats off to you and your love!'

Anamika didn't talk much but her smile said everything. She hugged Anurag and planted a kiss on his cheek and Anurag responded with a kiss on her forehead.

Anamika was a better and a stronger person today. She had true friends and her love by her side. Our entire life we search for that missing element in our life, we run behind materialistic things... Our life ends, but our search doesn't! Life could be much better if we search for love and run behind true friends. When I turned back to bid them goodbye, I saw a spark in her eyes. She was living again. I smiled and thought that things need to come to an end if they have to make way for a beautiful beginning. Everyone feels pain in their lives. One can either use that to become a better and a stronger person or use it as an excuse not to be one!

What next? I boarded my flight to Mumbai with memories of Mia Bella and all the people who were closely associated with VAYU.

Sakshi has now started visiting the rehab centre every weekend to check on Anamika. She has promised me that she will convey my best wishes to Anamika whenever she pays her a visit. She is a true friend and I know she will never break her promise. True friends are those who talk without intention, love without condition, care without expectation, and use cuss words without reason! I was blessed to have a few friends like her in my life.

I boarded the flight and switched on my iPod.

'Naseeba Naseeba…ye meri life hai…naseeba naseeba… tanha kyu ye dil hai…'

I had downloaded the tracks of VAYU and listening to the songs reminded me of Vikrant's story and that one evening in Mia Bella…

In every girl's life, there is a boy she'll never forget and in every boy's life, there is a girl he'll never forget. Anamika, Yuvi, and Vikrant too had someone in their lives. But sometimes you need pain and heartache to see what matters most. No one can ever understand your pain until they are put in your position. They had decided to stop re-reading the same chapter of their lives as with the next chapter, the story was bound to get better. Happy endings do exist…it all depends on where you end the story.

Acknowledgements

A lot of great things have happened in my life since the release of *Few Things Left Unsaid* (2011), *That's the Way We Met* (2012) and *It Started With a Friend Request* (2013). I would like to thank everybody who trusted me and supported me selflessly. I thank my millions of readers all over the world for their unconditional love and support. You all mean the world to me!

All the people I thank below have been my motivation while I finished writing the manuscript. I hope I hit the bull's eye with this one too.

To Vikrant and Anamika for permitting me to share their story and for fearlessly backing me to bring their story to life. Thanks for sharing your life story with me that night in Delhi, or this book wouldn't have been possible. I hope I have done justice to your story. A special thanks to Sakshi for showing patience and convincing Vikrant. I have no words to thank Anuj, the manager of Mia Bella, who allowed us to sit there for as long as we wanted.

To Dipika Tanna and Jasmine Sethi for being my strength, handling my mood swings, calming me down when I'm angry, and motivating me to write better.

To Mrunmayee Ambekar for honest reviews and for supporting me, Saurabh More for boosting my morale, Apurva for her guidance throughout, Priyanka Dhasade for reading the script inspite of her busy schedule, Neha Maheshwari and Mrunmayi Dhurandar for selflessly promoting my work, and Rashmi for praising me every time.

Thanks also to Madhwi and Vandana for being their cute selves and for understanding my emotions.

Thank you Zankrut Oza, Narendra Singh, Manik Jaiswal, and RJ Jeeturaaj for their selfless promotions.

To the people who really matter—mom, dad, and my sister Shweta for their humble support. Love you all!

Thank you to my grandparents—Sulbha and Divakar Palimkar—for your constant blessings.

To God, for being kind to me when it comes to my writing.

My extended family on Facebook and Twitter.

Thanks to Milee Ashwarya, Gurveen Chadha, Shruti Katoch, and the entire team at Random House India for always answering my crazy questions.

Lastly, a big thank you to my growing family of readers. Love you forever and hamesha!

A Note on the Author

Sudeep Nagarkar is the author of three bestselling novels—*Few Things Left Unsaid* (2011), *That's the Way We Met* (2012), and *It Started With a Friend Request* (2013).

All his books are inspired from real-life incidents and continue to top the bestseller charts. He was awarded a Youth Achiever's Award in 2013.

He has a degree in Electronics Engineering from Mumbai University and has completed management studies from Welingkar Institute of Management. He is also a motivational speaker and has given guest lectures in various reputed institutes and organizations.